"Look, Dad,

What was Renee doing here? Filling in for another volunteer, she told him when she entered the amusement park.

So he wasn't the only one she helped in her job.

Seeing the way Renee smiled down at his sons told him he wanted to be more than part of her job.

"Hey, Dad, can I go with my friends and our teacher?" Owen asked.

Rhys bit back the *no* that sprang to his lips and stifled his disappointment. His son would have more fun with his friends, and that was what this day was about.

"How about you, Dylan?" he asked his other boy. "Do you want to go with your friend?"

"No. I like being with Miss Renee. It's kind of like being with Mommy."

Rhys swallowed hard. In some ways, it was how things might have been for Dylan in their family if he hadn't messed up. In other ways, it wasn't at all the same. He and Renee… He didn't know what their relationship was. But one thing was certain. He wanted to find out.

Jean C. Gordon's writing is a natural extension of her love of reading. From that day in first grade when she realized *t-h-e* was the word *the*, she's been reading everything she can put her hands on. Jean and her college-sweetheart husband share a 175-year-old farmhouse in Upstate New York with their daughter and her family. Their son lives nearby. Contact Jean at Facebook.com/jeancgordon.author or PO Box 113, Selkirk, NY 12158.

Books by Jean C. Gordon

Love Inspired

Reuniting His Family

The Donnelly Brothers

Winning the Teacher's Heart
Holiday Homecoming
The Bachelor's Sweetheart

Small-Town Sweethearts
Small-Town Dad
Small-Town Mom
Small-Town Midwife

Reuniting His Family

Jean C. Gordon

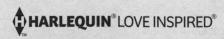

Recycling programs
for this product may
not exist in your area.

LOVE INSPIRED BOOKS

ISBN-13: 978-0-373-89947-0

Reuniting His Family

Copyright © 2017 by Jean Chelikowsky Gordon

www.Harlequin.com

Printed in U.S.A.

The Lord takes care of those
who are as helpless as children.
When I was in great need, He saved me.
—*Psalms* 116:6

To my critique partners, Chris and Bonnie,
for aiding my research for this book with
their invaluable knowledge of the New York State
foster care, family court and social services system.

Chapter One

Rhys Maddox looked across the small room at his broken dream. The dream he'd shattered. His boys stood in the doorway with a woman who wasn't their mother. Owen was a miniature copy of himself. Dylan had so many of his mother's features, it made his heart bleed.

"Mr. Maddox?"

He looked at Renee Delacroix, the Essex County Child Protection Services' worker he'd been sitting with.

"This is Suzanne Hill, Owen and Dylan's foster mother," she said.

Rhys strangled the shudder that began when the word *foster* formed on Ms. Delacroix's lips. Those memories were behind him and would be behind his boys soon, too. He stood and offered the woman his hand, glad for the opportunity to break away from Ms. Delacroix's scrutiny and the knowledge that she stood between him and his sons.

"Mrs. Hill," he said, warmed by her wholesome freshness, a contrast to Ms. Delacroix's glacial beauty. "It's good to meet you in person."

"Suzi, please," she said, smiling.

"Suzi, then."

Today's half hour with the Child Services' worker was his second meeting with Ms. Delacroix since he'd come to Paradox Lake to claim his sons. Yet they were still Mr. Maddox and Ms. Delacroix.

He released Suzi's hand. "May I?" he asked, glancing from Dylan to Owen, uncertain what he was asking for.

Suzi looked over his shoulder toward the table where he'd been sitting.

Ms. Delacroix must have given the okay.

He ruffled nine-year-old Owen's hair. "How's it going, buddy?"

They'd both grown since he'd seen them this spring at their mother's funeral. His gut ached. He'd missed so much the past five years.

Owen threw his arms around Rhys, almost knocking him over in excitement.

"Daddy, I'm so glad you're home. You're not going to have to go back again like you did after

Mommy's..." The rest of Owen's words were muffled against Rhys's chest.

He rested his head on his older son's. "No." *Never.*

No way was he going to let anything get between him and his responsibility to his family again. He set Owen back and looked into his face. "I'm so proud of you, helping your mom and taking care of Dylan for me. Mrs. Hill sent me your soccer game pictures and one of your winning Pinewood Derby car. And I kept all of the Bible verses that you and Dylan memorized in Sunday school and wrote out for me."

"Coach Josh helped me with the car. I painted it like your old Charger. This year, you and me can make one and win first prize instead of second."

Rhys's throat clogged. "Sure thing." He lifted his hands from Owen's shoulders and squatted in front of his younger son. "How about you, Dylan? Want to go get some ice cream with Daddy?"

"No." The six-and-a-half-year-old shook his head emphatically. "You're a bad man. My friend Tyler said so. His mommy told him."

Dylan's words hit him harder than Owen's near tackle. Dylan had been only a toddler when Rhys had been sent to Dannemora Correctional Facility for his part as the getaway driver in a bank robbery. The little guy didn't remember the four of them as a family, the home they'd had in Albany. But Gwen had brought both of the boys to Dannemora to see him as often as she could manage.

"Dylan. This is Daddy. It'll be fun." Owen jumped to his defense, filling Rhys with regret for all of the times his older son and Gwen had had to cover for him because he hadn't been there, due to his pride, bad choices and plain stupidity.

"No, I don't have to go. Ms. Delacroix said so. Right, Mrs. Hill?"

Rhys followed Dylan's gaze from him to Suzi and caught her look of pity before she hid it. He stood and spun around, glaring at Renee Delacroix. She looked barely old enough to be out of college. She was an intern, and *she* had the authority to keep his son from him? He fisted his hands.

Ms. Delacroix avoided his glare and fixed her gaze on his fists. "Dylan expressed some reluctance to go with you today. I assured him that he didn't have to if he didn't feel secure."

Security was one of the many things he'd failed to provide his family. His anger seeped out, combating his rigid stance.

"Transitioning can be more difficult for some children," she said.

Transitioning? Rhys worked his jaw. He was Dylan's father. He wanted to take his sons for a soft-serve ice-cream cone, with supervision, of course. The plan had been for Mrs. Hill to take the boys and meet him at the ice-cream stand on Paradox Lake, near her home and the house he'd rented.

Ms. Delacroix pushed away from the table and walked over to stand next to Rhys, facing Dylan. A faint aroma, sweet and floral, tickled his senses. Was it her shampoo? He eyed her black hair pulled back in some kind of fancy braid with a few wispy curls escaping around her face. He knew she couldn't be as young as she looked. When she'd introduced herself, she'd said she was a graduate student interning with the county. She'd mentioned mission work she'd done with children in Haiti before coming to work in Social Services.

"Dylan, if I go with your daddy to get ice cream, do you want to come or do you want to stay with Mrs. Hill?" Ms. Delacroix asked.

While he waited for his son to answer, Rhys followed one of her curls along the curve of her cheek. He curled his lip against the bitter tang in his mouth. What had gotten into him, besides having been incarcerated with 2,500 men for the past five years? He was here for Dylan and Owen, to make them a family again. Not to be distracted by and wonder about Renee Delacroix.

Dylan wrapped his arms around his foster mother's leg. "I want to go home with Mrs. Hill."

Home. With a woman Dylan had only known for a matter of months. This wasn't the dream that had kept him going since Gwen's death, while he was waiting for his appeal and release.

"I want to go with you, Dad." Owen's voice pulled him from the dark place he was headed.

"You still can," Ms. Delacroix said. "I can come and drive you back to the Hills' house afterward."

"Would that be all right with you, Dad?"

"More than all right." He'd take whatever he could get when it came to spending time with his sons.

Rhys nodded to Ms. Delacroix. "I know it's part of your job, but thanks for going out of your way." He scuffed the toe of his work boot on the floor. The drive from Elizabethtown, where the Social Services' office was located, to Paradox Lake and back would take her more than an hour. "I mean, having to take Owen home afterward and coming back here."

"It's no problem." A true smile spread across her face, the first the all-business lady had given him. "I live near Paradox Lake. You can wait here with Mrs. Hill while I go back to my office and wrap things up so we can go."

"Sure." He'd been waiting five years to be with his boys. What were a few more minutes?

"Go ahead and sit." Renee's hand accidentally brushed Rhys Maddox's biceps as she motioned toward a couch and chairs near the table. The rock-hard resistance unsettled her. She rushed out into the hall. *Let him think I'm hurrying to get back for the visitation, not to get away from him.*

Maybe she was too much of a newbie at this work but everything about Rhys Maddox unsettled her—from his record and conviction, to his tall, dark, imposing stature, to his icy-blue eyes that had thawed only when he spoke to Owen and Dylan. Especially his eyes. They weren't just cold. They were devoid of light.

Renee crossed her arms to counteract a shiver. She was authorized to oversee supervised visits and knew how overloaded the Maddox family's caseworker was. It wasn't as if she was to decide whether or not to place his children with him. But she hated taking on responsibilities she wasn't sure she was qualified to handle, making decisions like the ones she'd had to make in Haiti because the mission had been so understaffed. A week from Monday—the start of her new job as a Building Bridges' facilitator for the Christian Action Coalition—couldn't come soon enough. There she'd be working primarily with kids in child care and after-school programs, helping them adjust to changed family situations—divorce, death of a parent, a parent marrying or remarrying.

Renee checked with the caseworker to see if she wanted to handle the visit herself. It *was* Rhys Maddox's first visit. And receiving the "no" answer she'd expected, Renee headed to her office. She scanned her desk to make sure anything that should be secured in the file cabinets was tucked away and walked back to the visitation room.

Renee heard the rumble of Rhys's voice as she approached the doorway, but couldn't make out his words.

"Ready?" she asked as she stepped inside. Her cheery greeting bounced off the tense silence in the room. Owen sat next to his father, tapping his foot on the floor as if he couldn't wait to go. Dylan had curled up on Suzi's lap in a chair, his face buried in his foster mother's shoulder. Their father was soldier-straight on the couch, his hands clamped on his thighs.

"I asked him how his reading was coming. Gwen…" Rhys paused to swallow. "My wife had told me how excited Dylan was about starting to recognize words, that it looked like he was going to be a reader like she was. She read everything."

"Yeah," Owen piped up. "Dylan's really good

at reading. I had some trouble with it at my old school, but Mrs. Bradshaw helped me last year."

Rhys's gaze flickered between his sons. He pinched his lower lip and released it as if he was going to say something. But he didn't.

Renee filed a mental reminder to note in the records that, with his father gone, Owen may have adopted a protective, man-of-the-family stance with his mother and brother that he was extending to his father now. Rhys's stony expression implied that could cause conflict between Rhys and Owen. Both her earlier interview with Rhys and talking with him today had given her the distinct impression that he was a man who would protect his own, who wouldn't welcome outside assistance, maybe not even from his eldest son.

"Are you sure you don't want to go for ice cream?" Suzi lifted Dylan and placed him on the floor between her legs. "I'll come."

The little boy shook his head. Suzi gave her and Rhys a look that said *I tried*.

"I'll talk to you tomorrow, Mrs. Hill. 'Bye, Dylan," Renee said.

"'Bye, son."

Rhys's tone had no inflection, as if he were afraid the boy would detect any emotion as he spoke. Emotion that had far too much of an impact on Renee. Despite her training and all her work with disrupted families in Haiti, she still had a hard time comprehending a child wanting to shut out a parent or parent shutting out a child, even if there was a good reason. Her frame of reference always came back to her big, boisterous, loving family.

Dylan took Suzi's hand. "'Bye," he said, not looking at either her or Rhys.

Rhys cleared his throat. "Owen says there's a stand on the lake that serves soft ice cream. He'd like to go there."

"I know the one. My family and I go there all the time."

Rhys rose and Owen hopped off the couch.

"Do you have kids, Ms. Delacroix?" Owen asked as she led them from the room toward the back door.

"No, but I have two brothers—one's my twin—and three sisters, three nieces, a nephew and another niece or nephew on the way."

"Wow! I have only Dylan…and my dad. But Mrs. Hill's mother told me she would be my grandmother 'cause I don't have any grandmas or any grandpas."

Rhys locked his jaw and pushed the door so it swung open hard, almost banging against the brick wall of the building. He held himself back until they were out and almost down the sidewalk before exiting.

"My dad doesn't have any parents. He had parents, but he doesn't know them. He had foster parents like the Hills. Lots of them."

Renee nodded. That information had been in Rhys's records.

"My mom's parents don't like us."

Rhys caught up with them.

"But we don't care about that, do we, Dad?"

From the fire in his father's eyes, the man might care. She knew Gwen Maddox had been estranged from her parents. Renee's brother-in-law, Connor Donnelly, pastor at the Hazardtown Community Church, had called Gwen's parents to inform them of her death and funeral, and they'd practically hung up on him. When he'd said the boys were being placed in temporary foster care, their grandmother had started to say something but their grandfather had cut her off, telling Connor, "Foster care was good enough for their father. It's good enough for them."

"I've got you and Dylan." Rhys wrapped his arm around his son and squeezed his shoulder. "What more could I want?"

"Mom."

Rhys sucked in a breath. "Your mother."

Owen looked over the parking lot. "Which car is yours, Dad?"

"I have a pickup. For work."

At their earlier interview, he'd said he was looking for construction or electrical work but hadn't found anything. Had Rhys heard something since then? He hadn't said anything today.

"Mrs. Hill's husband has a F-350 pickup with a supercab so Dylan's booster seat fits and we can ride with Mr. Hill in the back seat. And he has a tow truck. That's what he does, tows cars and fixes them."

Owen's words made Rhys wince. "Sounds like a man I should get to know."

"Yeah, you'd like Mr. Hill," Owen said. "Maybe you can be friends."

Renee followed Rhys's gaze across the parking lot to a compact pickup with faded red paint and a missing hubcap, and understood the meaning of his comment.

"Ms. Delacroix, Mrs. Hill said I had to ride with you, but couldn't I go with my dad? I can show him where we're going, or you can drive first and we'll follow."

"No, son," Rhys answered for her. "We have to follow the rules, so we can all live together again. I'll follow Ms. Delacroix."

His words shouted control, which she read as another indication he'd do *whatever* he had to do to have his boys. Again, she was thankful she'd be done with her internship with Social Services soon, and that this would be the extent of her getting between him and his sons. It might be a flashback to her experience in Haiti, but Rhys

Maddox struck her as a complex man—a man whom, despite the draw of his obvious love and devotion to his sons, she might not want to get on the wrong side of.

The truck didn't start with his first two turns of the key and he could see Ms. Delacroix sitting in her car in the driving lane in front of him, chalking up more demerits against him. *No job. No reliable transportation. No good for Owen and Dylan.* He snorted a laugh. He'd been hearing the no-good part his whole life, from everyone but Gwen and the praise ministry and his Bible study group at Dannemora. He rested his head on the steering wheel for a moment before trying a third time. The engine rattled into action.

He'd get something better once he started working and could afford payments. He was trying to spend as little as possible of the money from Gwen's life insurance policy through the school district where she'd worked. That money was for Owen and Dylan's future. The first and last month's rent and security deposit on the three-bedroom house he'd rented on Hazard Cove Road had taken a sizable chunk. The house was a financial stretch, but it reminded him of the house he and Gwen had had in Albany. Their home. Another casualty of his rash actions.

Ms. Delacroix tooted her car horn to signal

she was taking off. He followed close behind for the thirty-mile trip to Paradox Lake and then to the opposite side of the lake from his rental house. She pulled into a rustic, old-fashioned, ice-cream stand. A red-and-white candy-striped awning shielded the order window from the hot midafternoon sun. Several picnic tables sported matching umbrellas.

Owen was out of Ms. Delacroix's car and over to his truck almost before he'd shut it off—with the cooperation of the engine.

"Is vanilla still your favorite, Dad? Mine's still chocolate. Can I have my cone dipped in chocolate, too?"

"Anything you want." *This time.* He'd have to watch himself to avoid indulging the boys to make up for lost time. It was a recommendation Ms. Delacroix had made that he couldn't argue with, even though he wanted to give them the best of everything.

He stepped up to the window. "We'll have a large chocolate-dipped."

Owen grinned at him, warming his heart in a way he hadn't felt in a long time. *Too long.*

"A large vanilla-dipped and…" Rhys turned to Renee.

"You don't have to pay for mine," she said. "I'll get my own."

"No, I'm treating."

She shifted her weight from one foot to the other. "I can't accept. It's a CPS rule. We can't take gifts." She placed her order.

Another rule. He fingered the bills in his hand. He could accept it. The past five years had made him a master at accepting rules.

"Hey, Dad," Owen said as they started toward an empty picnic table, "that's my friend Alex and his dad. Can we sit with them?"

Rhys's eyes followed Owen's outstretched arm to a table where a dark-haired man and a boy about his son's age sat eating burgers. He fought back a frown. This was supposed to be his time with his boys. Dylan had refused to come and now Owen wanted to be with his friend.

He took the easy out. "Ms. Delacroix?"

"It's up to you."

If it was up to him, he wouldn't be here now at all. Owen and Dylan would both be living with him already.

Owen looked at him expectantly, with his mother's eyes.

"Sure," Rhys said.

Ms. Delacroix's smile of approval lifted the gray mantle settling on him as much as Owen's did.

He was pathetic, waiting for validation of everything he did.

Let go and let God. He'll make everything

right. Except Rhys's faith was so new, he wasn't sure he knew how to let go yet.

"Hey, Owen," his friend Alex called.

"Hi," Owen called back, tugging Rhys toward the table. "This is my dad," he said as they approached the table.

Rhys's insides went mushy at the pride in his son's voice. He certainly hadn't done much to make him proud in the past. But that was behind him. He wouldn't let Owen or Dylan down again.

"Rhys Maddox." He extended his hand over the table to Alex's father.

"Neal Hazard." He stood and shook hands. "Hi, Renee," Neal said before sitting again. "Looks like you two are joining us." He motioned to the bench beside him, where Owen was already seated next to Alex.

"Hi." She stepped around Rhys to sit on the bench across from Neal.

Ms. Delacroix and Neal seemed friendly, even though Neal had to be ten or fifteen years older than her. Not that it mattered to him.

Rhys sat on the opposite end of the bench across from Owen.

"Just you and Alex today?" Renee glanced toward the stand.

"Yep. Anne and Sophia are having a girls' day shopping for school clothes and Ian's at soccer camp. I took the afternoon off so Alex wouldn't have to go shopping with his mother and sister."

"A fate worse than death, for sure," Renee said.

Neal laughed in agreement, making Rhys wish he could pull off the easy manner Neal had with her.

"Maddox," Neal said mid-laugh, as if he'd suddenly realized who Rhys was.

Rhys tensed, waiting for the other man to make the connection between him and the CPS worker.

"I should have put it together."

Anger started to simmer in the pit of Rhys's stomach. Hazard had better not say anything bad about him in front of Owen.

"You're the guy who rented one of the old summer houses from my dad."

Rhys squirmed on the bench. He wouldn't be doing his boys any good if he was always on the defensive, expecting the worst from everyone.

"Yes, if your father is Ted Hazard." Rhys could see a resemblance.

"Sure is. I don't know why I didn't think of Owen when Dad told me. We're neighbors. Our house is right around the corner off Hazard Cove Road. Alex and Owen are almost inseparable. It'll save us a lot of driving if they're within walking distance of each other."

Rhys looked at his son, who was in deep conversation with his friend. "Owen will like that. I hope to have him and Dylan with me soon."

Neal nodded without asking for any further explanation.

He knows. Of course, he knows. Neal's kid was Owen's best friend.

Rhys's stomach muscles clenched. Neal seemed to know Ms. Delacroix well enough to know she worked for the county CPS. And when he'd rented the house, Rhys had given Neal's father full disclosure about his conviction and early release after new evidence had exonerated him of involvement in an earlier bank robbery—a robbery during which a bank guard had been shot. He wiped a drop of ice cream from his hand. How many other people knew of his background? What would that do to his job prospects? He didn't want to move the boys. Not right away. Gwen had said Paradox Lake was a good place, and he didn't want to disrupt Owen and Dylan's lives any more than necessary.

"I'm going to get some water," Renee said.

Rhys ran his tongue along the inside of dry lips. He could use one, too.

"Dad, can I get Coke?" Owen asked.

"Yes." Rhys reached in his jeans' pocket for his wallet. "And I'll have a water, if you don't mind."

"Not at all." She took his money. "Do you want anything, Neal?"

"We're good, but you'll need some help carrying the drinks."

"We'll help." Owen and Alex hopped off the bench.

"Good men," Neal said before focusing his attention on Rhys. "Dad said you're looking for work. You're an electrician?"

"I did most of an apprenticeship with the Brotherhood of Electrical Workers." Rhys bit back the "before" he'd been about to add. There was no need to bring up his past. "Do you have a lead on a job?"

"I'm looking for someone. I'm an electrical contractor. We do mostly solar installations and other work for my wife's company, GreenSpaces."

GreenSpaces, a big, international corporation, was on his list of places to check out. Rhys eyed Neal questioningly.

"Yeah." Neal laughed. "You look the same way I did when I first learned Anne was a bigwig corporate executive. She teaches engineering at North Country Community College, too."

"Your wife owns GreenSpaces?"

Neal nodded. "Anne and her first husband started the company, and she inherited his stock to add to her own when he died."

Rhys shifted on the hard wooden bench. "I'm not licensed or part of a union or anything," he said, wanting to be honest about his qualifications.

"The job I have is for a more general laborer, but your electrical knowledge is a plus. Interested?"

"I sure am." He saw no reason to hide his enthusiasm.

Neal reached in his wallet and pulled out his business card. "Does eight o'clock tomorrow morning work for you for an interview?"

"Eight's fine."

Rhys fingered the card. His roller-coaster life was heading up again. He prayed that it stayed there as he watched Owen walk back with Renee and thought about Dylan. CPS seemed to be more into keeping them apart than in reuniting them. He'd talk with Pastor Connor about the Building Bridges thing at the Hazardtown Community Church. Rhys had shrugged off the pastor's recommendation that he get involved to help him and his boys reconnect. But now he thought it just might help him reach Dylan—and keep the uphill momentum.

Chapter Two

Renee had trouble quelling the emotion that welled inside her as she watched father and son part ways in the driveway of the Hills' home. How did the other CPS workers maintain their professional distance? Would this be a problem at Building Bridges, too, working so closely with kids?

Owen began peppering his father with questions such as "When will I see you again? Can I come and see the house you got us?" and "When can Dylan and I come live with you?"

She listened as his father calmly answered, reassuring the boy that he was as anxious as Owen to be a family again, but not giving his son any direct answers that could mislead him. Rhys had asked her the same questions when they'd met before the visit. The only answer she'd had for him then was that the Family Court judge would make those decisions.

After giving his son a final hug, Rhys climbed into his truck and drove away. She walked Owen into the house.

"Did you have a good time?" Suzi asked.

"The best," Owen said. "Alex and his dad were there, too."

"Dylan's been waiting for you to come home. He's up in your room."

"Okay. I'll go so you can talk to Ms. Delacroix."

Renee and Suzi laughed.

"Too perceptive for his own good," Suzi said once he was gone. "Did you have a chance to ask Mr. Maddox—Rhys—about Sunday dinner?"

"No, I didn't even think of it."

The original plan had been for Suzi to invite him to dinner after the ice-cream outing if everything had gone well, which Renee thought it had—with Owen, at least. But the episode with Dylan at the Social Services office had prevented Suzi from going to get ice cream with Rhys and having the opportunity to ask.

"I'll call him tomorrow," Renee said. Her heart raced at the prospect of hearing his deep voice, a voice that held the same hint of danger as his eyes and posture. But observing him with

Owen, she'd seen a man who didn't match her earlier impressions.

"Or I can," Suzi offered.

"No, I'll do it." Suzi would have to call her or the Maddox's caseworker with the details anyway.

"Okay, let me know what he says. Although I think I already know what his answer will be."

Renee nodded. "Talk to you later."

She walked to her car, her pulse still skittering. What was she afraid of? This wasn't Haiti. It was only a phone call, and one he'd welcome.

A half hour later Renee arrived at the three-family house in Ticonderoga where she and her sister Claire had an apartment. Before unlocking the front door she retrieved their mail, including a large padded envelope for Claire that was wedged between the mailbox and the house siding.

"Hey. Is that what I think it is?"

Renee jumped.

Claire stood at the bottom of the porch steps. "I hope whatever thought you were lost in was a good one," she said.

Not really. The picture in her mind of Rhys leaving his son faded and her anxiety returned. She waved the padded envelope to divert Claire's attention. "You're expecting something from Texas A&M maybe?"

Claire broke into a wide smile. "You know I am." She grabbed the envelope and clutched it to her chest as Renee opened the door.

"After you," Renee said, smiling as she followed Claire up to their second-floor apartment. Maybe she should order in or take Claire out to celebrate and clear her mind of work.

"How does it look on me?" Claire asked, draping her newly earned Masters in Agricultural Development degree in front of her.

"Fabulous. It really matches your ivory complexion."

"Don't you think?" Claire lifted the paper closer to her face and tilted her head.

"I'm proud of you," Renee said. "And I know Mom and Dad are, too."

She *was* proud of Claire. Her sister had decided what she'd wanted—a hands-on position at the Cornell Experimental Farm, and to eventually work her way up to director—and she'd focused all of her energy on what she'd needed to do to get there. All of her siblings were like that.

"I really admire your drive."

"You're no slacker yourself," Claire said.

"But sometimes I feel like I am, like I have no direction. The rest of you all knew what you wanted to do and were on your way there by the time you were my age."

Beginning with her oldest sister, they'd all

achieved their dreams—mother, chef, newscaster. Even her twin, Paul, who'd wanted to take over the family dairy farm since he'd seen his first baby calf.

"You're on your way with your graduate work, the internship you're wrapping up and your new job."

Renee pushed her hair off her forehead. "I'm headed somewhere, but I'm not sure it's where I want to be or where I'm supposed to be headed."

"I knew something's been bothering you. Talk to me," Claire said, placing her degree on an end table and motioning Renee to sit.

Renee dropped onto the couch. "I got my BA in sociology because I wanted to help people. When I graduated, I thought my calling was health care, so I went to Haiti. It wasn't health care. But—" *for the most part*, she added silently "—I made a difference working with the families that came into the clinic. I came back *knowing* I wanted to work with children and their families."

"Now you don't?" Claire asked.

"I do, but my internship has showed me that I don't want to work in child protection services." She peered into her sister's sympathetic face. "I don't want the responsibility of taking a child from or placing a child back with a parent and having something go wrong with the placement."

Claire draped her arm around Renee's shoulder, making Renee feel all the more the baby of the family.

"You did everything you could have done with what happened in Haiti. You said so yourself."

Renee dropped her head to her chest and drew a deep breath. "Everything but heed a dying mother's warning. The girl went willingly with her father." *Just like Owen was ready to move right in with his father.* "She was too young to know better."

"You did everything within your power," Claire reassured her. "You couldn't have known what would happen."

"So, I'm home and back to square one, trying to figure out what I want to be when I grow up. Ending my internship earlier than planned to change my job focus again, and throwing money away on a degree I may not use."

"Are you saying you think you should stay at CPS through August now, finish the internship?" Claire asked.

"No." Renee sighed. "But what if the Action Coalition and Building Bridges isn't my place, either? Didn't any of you have second or third thoughts about what you wanted to do?"

Claire wavered. "I can only speak for myself, but no. Sorry. A lot of people go through several 'first' jobs before settling into a career, though. You know we'll all be behind you, whatever you decide."

"Yes, I do." And maybe that was the problem. Her family members had always been right there to pick her up and set her on her feet, to baby her—even Paul.

Her thoughts skittered to Rhys Maddox, who had no one but himself to support him. Yet, through his barely concealed anger he'd radiated confidence in his ability to get custody of his sons.

Renee blew out a breath with a whoosh that made Claire look at her. It was about time she stood on her own two feet—and her faith—and made a plan with no one holding her hand.

Rhys strode up to the oversize barn-style garage set across the driveway from a large log home. Neal Hazard hadn't been exaggerating when he'd said they were neighbors. The house and garage office were well within walking distance from the house he was renting on Hazard Cove Road. The buildings, nestled in the thick pinewoods that lined both sides of the private road, weren't visible from the main road.

He slapped the bright red folder he clenched in his right hand against his leg. He'd worn black chinos and a dress shirt—his only dress shirt—for the interview, but had had to settle for his new work boots. They'd seemed a better choice than his athletic shoes.

Although he'd used the library to apply on-line for a dozen other jobs, this was his first interview. He turned the doorknob and pushed the door open, not sure what to expect.

Neal's office looked like any guy's garage with the addition of a desk pushed back in the corner, facing the door. "Right on time," Neal said, looking over the computer monitor in front of him. "Come in, sit down."

He took a seat in the chair to the left of the desk, and Neal swiveled to face him head-on. Rhys placed the red folder on the desk and pushed it toward Neal. "My résumé."

Neal handed him a paper in exchange. "Our job application. You can write 'on résumé' for previous employment."

Rhys pulled a pen from his shirt pocket and went to work on the application, shutting down the urge to look up at Neal's expression while he reviewed his résumé.

"How much of the apprenticeship had you completed when you…" Neal paused, as if searching for the right word.

"Before I was arrested," Rhys finished for him. No sense in tiptoeing around the facts. He'd done his time for his actions. Actions he no longer justified with needing to make back payments on their mortgage and taxes to avoid his family ending up homeless. He knew now that he'd broken God's commandment, and had asked for and received forgiveness. "I had about three and a half years of the apprenticeship done. I've reapplied to pick up the Associate of Applied Science degree in general technology I was pursuing online as part of the apprenticeship."

"Good."

Rhys finished the application and looked up.

"I can contact your references for more information?" Neal asked, tapping the letter from the electrician who'd supervised Rhys's work in Albany.

"About my work, yes." The electrician had assured Rhys he'd have no problem discussing with potential employers the progress he'd made in the apprenticeship program.

"And Connor Donnelly? You participated in his ministry at Dannemora?"

"I—"

"Wait, you don't have to answer. I shouldn't have asked."

"No, I put it in the references. I have no problem talking about it." If Neal was going to hold his faith against him in any way, he wasn't a person Rhys wanted to work for, despite how badly he needed work. "I'm indebted to Pastor Connor for leading me to Christ and for helping Gwen, my wife, relocate here so I could see her and the boys more." Rhys leaned forward. "And Owen and Dylan are registered for The Kids Place summer and after-school child-care program at Connor's church when CPS gives the go-ahead for them to live with me."

Neal raised his hand in a sign of surrender and Rhys's heart dropped. Him and his big mouth. Gwen had always said he didn't talk much, but when he had something to say, he had no filter.

"Hey, I know where you're coming from. I was a single father for nineteen years."

Rhys leaned back.

"My oldest daughter, Autumn, was born when I was seventeen, and she was practically my whole life until she graduated high school. She and Pastor Connor were classmates. Autumn's a midwife at the birthing center in Ticonderoga. I raised her myself. Granted, I had help from my mom and dad, but she was my responsibility."

"So you understand." Rhys accepted the kinship Neal offered. That's what he planned to do: make Owen and Dylan the center of his life. He couldn't imagine marrying again, as Neal had, or having more kids. He owed his boys too much to have anything left over for anyone else.

"But you're probably more interested in knowing about the job than my kids," Neal said.

Rhys kept a rein on his excitement as Neal

outlined the responsibilities of the position, but almost lost it when he heard the generous starting salary.

"Any questions?" Neal asked when he'd finished.

Rhys hesitated. "Health insurance?" He didn't care so much for himself, but he needed it for the boys. It would be another positive he could report to CPS.

"Good insurance. Better than most small employers can offer. It's through GreenSpaces' multi-company plan. And we have a retirement savings plan, too."

He tried to look appreciative. For now, all he wanted was to be able to make a secure home for his family.

"Anything else?" Neal asked.

"Not that I can think of."

"All right, then." Neal rose.

Rhys followed suit. "Thank you for the opportunity to interview."

"I'll give you a call within the next couple of days. If your references check out, you have the job." Neal smiled. "Anyone else in the area with your training and experience already works for me."

"I look forward to hearing from you." Rhys walked out of the office at a controlled pace, rather than bounding to the door in leaps of joy, as he wanted to. He couldn't imagine either his former supervisor or Pastor Connor telling Neal anything derogatory about him. He whistled his way to his truck, which started with the first turn of the key. Nothing could dampen his spirits.

His cell phone vibrated in his pocket and Rhys pulled it out and saw the CPS number.

Well, almost nothing.

"Is that him?" Owen asked Renee for the third time in the past five minutes.

She went to the front window, pushed back the curtain and spotted Rhys's truck slowing to turn into the Hills' driveway. She brushed her moist palms against the skirt of her black-and-white crinkle-cotton summer dress.

"Yes, your dad is pulling in the driveway."

Owen reached the door at the same time Rhys knocked.

"You're supposed to ask before you open the door, Owen," Dylan said. "Mrs. Hill said so. It could be a stranger."

"It's Dad. Ms. Delacroix said so." Owen looked over his shoulder at Renee.

"Go ahead."

Owen swung the door open. "You're here."

A broad smile spread across Rhys's face, softening the angular, almost harsh edges of his features.

"Of course I'm here. I told you at church this morning I would be."

"I know, but I'm just so glad."

"Me, too." Rhys moved his gaze from Owen to Dylan, who stood next to Renee but edged closer. Rhys's smile faltered a bit. "Hi, Dylan."

"Hi, Daddy," Dylan said before turning his face into the side of her leg.

"Ms. Delacroix."

"Hi. The boys have been checking every few minutes to see if you were here yet." She was only slightly exaggerating. Owen had been checking enough for both of them.

"Yeah, we have a bunch of stuff to show you," Owen said.

"And I want to see it all. Give me a minute with Ms. Delacroix and to check in with the Hills." He glanced around the living room as if he'd just noticed they weren't there.

"Boys," she said. "Why don't you go into the kitchen and get those cookies you made for your dad, and the milk and paper cups?"

Owen looked from her to his father. "So you can tell Dad about the Hills?"

Something flickered in his father's eyes. If it was anyone else, she would call it fear, but she couldn't imagine him being afraid of anything or anyone.

"Can I carry the milk?" Dylan asked into her skirt.

She said yes and Dylan loosened his clutch. The boys ran off into the next room.

"I didn't expect to see you here," Rhys said. "I mean, the other day when you called, you said dinner at the Hills with the boys." He straightened, looming over her. "Where *are* the Hills?"

"It's nothing bad."

He knitted his eyebrows.

Great. Now she had him on edge. Not what she wanted. Her job should have been simple enough—be there in the background with him and the boys until Jack got back.

"On their way home from church, Suzi got a call from her grandmother's neighbor in Saranac Lake. Her grandmother took a fall this morning. She's all right. Nothing broken, but she's shaken up. Suzi drove up there and is staying with her for the afternoon."

"And Jack?"

"He got a towing call about an hour ago. He should be back any time now."

Rhys scrutinized her. "So you had to come and cover for them."

"I volunteered." Her internship wasn't just a job. She cared about the children. The people she worked with did, too. "The Hills didn't want to cancel and disappoint you and the boys."

"Ms. Delacroix, look at how strong I am." Dylan entered the room, lifting the gallon jug of milk for her to see and filling the silence that had stretched between her and his father.

She felt the pain that flickered across the man's face at his younger son turning to her, not him, for approval.

Owen followed with a plate of four cookies and cups. "Dylan, put the milk on the table before you drop it." He placed the cookies on the coffee table next to the jug. "Ms. Delacroix said we could only have one each so we don't spoil our appetite for dinner. We're having lasagna with meatballs."

"We certainly wouldn't want to spoil our appetites for that," Rhys said.

"I told Mrs. Hill that it's your favorite," Owen said.

"Me, too," Dylan said, grabbing his cookie and jumping up on the couch.

Rhys gave the boys a thumbs-up, sat on the couch next to, but not touching, his youngest son and poured him a cup of milk.

It was good to see Dylan interacting with his father. Maybe she'd imagined Rhys's resentment earlier. It might have been nerves. As stoic as he seemed, Rhys Maddox was human.

"Come on, Ms. Delacroix," Owen said, sidling up next to his father to make room for her on the couch. "There's space for you, too."

"In a minute. I need to check the lasagna." *And give your father a moment with you.* "I'd better stir the sauce and meatballs, too. I told Mr. Hill I wouldn't let it burn."

"We wouldn't want burned sauce, would we, guys?" Rhys asked.

"No!" the boys shouted.

From the stove, she could see directly across the kitchen and dining room to where they were in the living room. "I'll be right back."

Rhys nodded in her direction as he listened to Owen give a play-by-play of baking the cookies with Mrs. Hill.

In the kitchen, Renee lifted the lid of the saucepan and breathed in the spicy tomato smell. After giving the sauce a stir, she looked over her shoulder into the living room. Owen was still talking. She opened the oven and checked the lasagna. Silence from the other room made her spin around, heart pounding. The oven door snapped shut. *They were still there.* Relief flooded her. *Of course they were.* Rhys Maddox wouldn't do anything stupid to jeopardize his regaining custody.

"Everything looks good," she said as she re-entered the living room. "The timer's set for the lasagna. Mr. Hill should be back by the time it's done."

"Eat your cookie, Ms. Delacroix," Owen said. "We want to show Dad our room and stuff."

"Yeah," Dylan said. "Mrs. Hill said you'd stay right with us."

His father stiffened against the back of the couch.

"I can wait on the cookie. I know you're anxious to show your dad your things."

Owen leaped off the couch and grabbed his father's hand, pulling him toward the stairway. "Our room is upstairs."

"Wait for your brother," Rhys said.

Dylan slid off the couch. "I'll show you, Ms. Delacroix." He slipped his hand in hers.

Rhys's shoulders slumped for a moment. Straightening, he said, "Lead the way Owen."

Upstairs in the boys' room, Renee relaxed as they caught their father up on what they were doing in their lives. Their exuberant—and their father's more restrained—joy flowed over her, drawing her in.

"And this is my shirt drawer," Owen said once he ran out of other things to show his father.

The sound of the stove timer startled Renee away from the adoring grin on Rhys's face that had captivated her. He was a different person around Owen and Dylan.

"Hello? Where is everyone?" came a voice from below before she could excuse herself to check the pasta.

"That's Mr. Hill. I'll tell him you're here, Dad."

Owen raced down the stairs with Dylan shadowing him.

Their father stopped halfway down. "Before we have dinner, I have a question."

"Certainly, Mr. Maddox." She reassumed her professional demeanor that she'd let slip watching him and the boys.

"If we're going to be doing this visitation stuff…" He waved down the stairs. "Can you call me Rhys?"

"I can." Despite her best effort, she'd already started thinking of him as Rhys. "And please call me Renee, except in front of the boys." Not that she expected to have much contact with him and his sons once she started her new job a week from Monday.

"Gotcha," he said with the same smile that had softened her when he'd used it with his sons upstairs. The smile that cracked his armor and showed the dichotomy of Rhys Maddox—both the off-putting, cold, aloof male and the adoring father who tugged at her heartstrings.

Her departure from CPS couldn't come too soon.

Chapter Three

Rhys put his washed lunch dishes in the drainer and wiped the table down for the second time today. After three days of rain and being trapped inside—except for a couple times when the clouds had broken and he'd casually driven by the Hills' in hopes of catching a glimpse of Owen and Dylan—he had to get out.

He tossed the dishcloth into the sink. No, it hadn't been casual, but more stalker-like. He'd better be careful or he could mess things up. It didn't help that it had been almost a week and he hadn't heard from Neal Hazard about the job, nor had he heard from any of the places he'd applied to online.

The only bright spot had been his conversation with Pastor Connor. He had given him more details about the Building Bridges program and said that Owen and Dylan were two of the children the local school district had recommended for The Kids Place program. Connor had also asked Rhys if he'd be interested in volunteering at the group's weekly meetings and events. Several of the other children recommended had no male role models in their families. Flattered that Pastor Connor would think him role model material, Rhys said he'd consider it and let Connor know before the meeting of volunteers and staff next week at the Christian Action Coalition office. While he wasn't sold that it was entirely his thing, it would give him more time with his sons.

Rhys changed into a pair of shorts and grabbed the towel from the bathroom. When he'd rented the house, Ted Hazard had said to feel free to use the family beach next to the Sonrise summer camp on Paradox Lake. It was early Thursday afternoon and most people would be working. He'd probably have the place to himself. A half hour of hard swimming might lift the weight of his situation off him for a while.

When Rhys walked onto the beach, he saw he wasn't alone. Renee sat on a blanket towel-drying her hair next to a woman he didn't recognize. Just the reminder he was trying to escape. He hadn't heard from her or anyone else at CPS about another visit all week. He started to turn back. The jog from the house had worn off some adrenaline. Then he changed his mind. He couldn't be a hermit, not if he wanted to make any kind of life for him and his sons. Rhys strode toward the women. Better to be on the offensive than the defensive.

"Hey," he called with what he hoped was a friendly wave. He couldn't tell from the look on Renee's face when she turned around. It bordered somewhere between surprise and alarm.

"Hi, Rhys." She composed herself and dropped the towel onto the blanket.

He spread his own towel a short distance away. "Ted Hazard said I had beach privileges as part of the rental." Rhys regretted his words as soon as they were out. He should have said "Nice day" or "How's the water?" He didn't have to justify his every action to her or anyone else.

"Hello," the other woman said. "Since Renee has seemed to have lost her manners, I'm her sister Claire."

"I was getting to introductions," Renee said. "Claire, this is Rhys Maddox." She hesitated, glancing out at the lake. "D—" The rest of her introduction was drowned out by the shout of a little boy about Dylan's age racing toward them. Renee's nephew? Rhys's lunch churned in his stomach when he saw Dylan right behind the boy.

"Aunt Claire, I left my goggles in your car," the boy said.

"Daddy, what are you doing here?" Dylan asked. Not the most welcoming greeting, but Rhys would take it. "I was going to swim. I didn't know you were here, either."

"You can swim with us," Dylan said.

"I'd like to." He looked at Renee for confirmation.

She frowned.

It had seemed like a reasonable request to him.

"I thought you didn't have a father," the other boy said.

"That was last year."

Dylan's words sliced through him. His son had been telling his friends he didn't have a father?

"I told you I did now. Daddy, this is my friend Robbie. He's not the one who said you're a bad guy."

"Hi." *That's a real confidence booster.*

Robbie was dancing back and forth on his toes in the sand. "Can we get the goggles now? I want to show Dylan the cool rocks on the bottom of the lake."

"Come on." Claire stood and led the boys to the parking area, leaving him alone with Renee.

"Swimming with Dylan wouldn't be breaking any rules, would it? You're here."

She squinted up at him, even though the sun had gone behind the clouds. "Swimming shouldn't be a problem."

Rhys emptied his pockets of his cell phone and wallet. He never went anywhere without identification. A seagull squawked above, breaking the dead silence. This was where he should make small talk, except he'd never been good with small talk before his incarceration, and he wasn't any better now.

"So, Robbie's your nephew? He and Dylan are friends?" *Real smooth.*

"Yes, they're in the same class at school."

Silence settled in again, and Rhys looked out over the lake. None too soon, Claire and the boys were back with the goggles.

"Who wants to swim?" Rhys asked.

"I do," both boys said.

"Race you," Rhys said, taking off at a pace the boys could match.

"You didn't tell me he's even more attractive up close," Rhys heard Claire say as the boys caught up with him.

He strained to hear Renee's low response, but the boys and the sound of a boat on the lake made it impossible. He hit the water and dived in, welcoming the cold jolt from the hot August heat. Thinking of Renee in any way other than a professional one felt like he was betraying Gwen. They'd had a good marriage, although their relationship had been strained after he'd gone to prison. But one thing he'd never faltered on was his love for his wife and his commitment to the sanctity of their marriage vows.

Any attraction he might feel toward Renee was superficial. She was a beautiful woman. But he'd learned the hard way not to make decisions based on impulse, and had no room in his life for anyone other than his kids.

When he surfaced, Dylan and Robbie met him with a splash to the face. He growled and tickled them both, inciting a new round of splashing. He couldn't express how good it was to see Dylan laughing and squealing with him.

"I'm cold," Dylan said after about fifteen minutes of play. He looked up at Rhys as if uncertain whether his dad would be angry with him if he got out of the water early.

Rhys hid his disappointment. "You can go back on the beach and warm up," he assured him. As much as he'd like more time with Dylan, ending the game happily on his son's terms was progress. "I'm going to swim some more."

"But you don't have a buddy. You're always supposed to have a buddy when you swim," Dylan said.

"You and Robbie can watch me from the beach."

"No, I'll tell Ms. Delacroix you want her to watch you. She's a better swimmer than we are." With that, Dylan and Robbie paddled away.

Rhys dunked himself as he thought of Dylan telling Renee he wanted her to keep an eye on him. He stroked to the middle of the lake, trying not to think about Renee watching him.

"Surprise! Happy birthday!"

Renee jumped back and pasted a smile on her face when she and Claire entered the lounge of the Hazardtown Community Church for the Twenty-/ Thirtysomethings group meeting the next evening. "I'll get you," she said under her breath so that only her sister could hear her. Claire had to be behind this. Her friends meant well. They didn't know she didn't like surprises. But Claire did. The family celebration yesterday on her actual birthday had been plenty.

"Not me." Claire propelled her into the lounge. "Blame Pastor Connor for this one."

"What?" Connor asked. "Natalie said you've always wanted a surprise birthday party."

Everyone laughed. One deep resonating chuckle drew her attention. She'd hoped to use the evening at the weekly Bible study and social time afterward to escape the pressure she'd been under to tie everything up at CPS before she left. But work, in the form of Rhys Maddox, had followed her.

"All right. Find a seat," Pastor Connor said.

The twelve or so people settled down, with Renee sitting several chairs away from Rhys.

"As I'm sure you noticed, we have a new potential member, Rhys Maddox. Claire or Abby, can you share your study guide?" Pastor Connor asked, looking from Renee's sister sitting on one side of Rhys to the woman on the other side.

"On it," Claire said, opening her guide and spreading it between her and Rhys before Abby could open her mouth.

Renee stared at Claire. What was she up to? Claire couldn't be interested in the man. He wasn't her sister's type. Claire liked men with polish. Rhys was more of a diamond in the rough. Too much work, in Renee's opinion. Not that she thought of him that way, as an eligible man. Nor did he think of her as eligible, either, from the professional contact she'd had with him.

"Some of you may know Rhys," Connor said. "But we'll go around and introduce ourselves anyway."

Renee shifted her gaze to the right of Claire. Rhys was looking directly at her. She lowered her eyes and caught him shuffling the sole of his athletic shoe against the wood flooring. *He was nervous.* That was a new side of him—her impression was that nothing fazed the man. Things angered him, yes, but didn't rattle him.

"Renee?" Connor said.

Jerked from her thoughts, Renee moved her gaze past her sister, who smirked, to Connor and back to Rhys.

"Rhys and I know each other." She smiled at the group, stopping at Rhys. His expression was neutral. Renee crossed her ankles. Had her tone sounded sharp rather than friendly? Connor had startled her. She uncrossed her legs. What did she expect from Rhys? One of those smiles he reserved for his boys? They might be on a first-name basis now, but it wasn't as if they were friends.

The introductions continued around the circle back to Pastor Connor, and the group plunged into its usual routine: an opening prayer, reading of the week's lesson and lively discussion. Renee sat back in her seat, listening more than participating. Although she didn't know why, Rhys's participation surprised her. He didn't say much, but when he commented, his few words were insightful and thought-provoking, moving the discussion in interesting directions.

"Okay," Connor said, "I'm going to wrap the meeting up now, so we can party."

Renee looked at the clock on the wall, surprised the hour had passed so quickly. Rhys's gaze snagged hers as she looked down again. A prickle ran down her spine.

"Jon," Conner asked one of the men, "will you do the closing prayer?"

Renee bowed her head while the words of the prayer rolled over her without really registering.

Afterward, the group members headed toward the door. Renee waited for her sister.

"The cleaning staff likes us to keep food in the church hall," she heard Claire tell Rhys. "It makes cleanup easier."

"I can't stay. Something's come up. I have a call I need to return." Rhys rested his hand on the phone clipped to his belt.

Claire frowned at his departing back.

"Happy birthday," he said as he brushed by Renee, leaving before she could say thanks. The relief she felt was as much for Rhys as for herself. No question about it, the man unsettled her. As for him, she guessed that a regular meeting would have been a better introduction to their group. By all indications, Rhys was a loner. She was sure he'd come expecting the Bible study Pastor Connor had probably told him about, not a birthday party for her.

The party wasn't as bad as she'd expected—it actually wasn't bad at all. Abby had baked her favorite German chocolate cake, and Pastor Connor's sister-in-law Becca pointed out that Renee was still the baby of the group.

"Hey," Claire said afterward as they drove home, "Rhys Maddox sure is Mr. Personality."

"What do you mean?"

Claire headed past the lake toward Ticonderoga. "He could have at least stayed for a piece of cake. Returning a phone call is a flimsy excuse for leaving."

"Not if it was about his kids."

"Wouldn't you have gotten a call from Suzi?"

"Maybe not." *Although probably.* "It could have been about a job." Renee didn't know why she was coming to Rhys's defense.

"A business call at this time of night? But I'll cut him some slack. He is take-your-breath-away handsome."

Renee couldn't argue with her sister. Rhys Maddox was striking. "Claire, you're not interested in him, are you?"

Claire parked the car in front of their apartment-house. "I don't know." She shrugged. "You know how I like a challenge."

Renee's shoulders tightened. Was it apprehension because her sister had no idea what she'd be getting with Rhys? Or something else altogether?

Rhys welcomed the cool breeze blowing off the lake when he stepped out of the church hall. Unless he was wrong, Renee's sister Claire had been showing interest in him. He ran his hand through his hair. She and the other woman who'd sat beside him had both been friendly, and Renee hadn't liked it. At least, she hadn't liked her sister being friendly. If he had a sister, he probably wouldn't want her being friendly with someone like him, either. And Renee hadn't looked any happier when he'd made his exit. Maybe she thought he was blowing her off by not staying for cake.

He shook off the thoughts of both Delacroix sisters and pulled his phone from his pocket. It had buzzed during the Bible discussion and he'd checked it to see if it was the Hills. It hadn't been, so he'd figured he could wait until after the meeting to check the voice mail.

He leaned against the cab of his truck and looked out at the pine forest as he now waited for the voice mail to connect.

"Rhys, this is Neal Hazard."

A film of dampness formed between his palm and the phone.

"Sorry about calling so late on a Friday. We're working out near Watertown, and I just got back. If you're still interested in the job, give me a call, anytime until nine tonight or during the day tomorrow."

Rhys checked the time: 8:52. Good thing he'd skipped the party. He wouldn't have been able to sleep tonight without knowing what Neal had to say. He quickly dialed Neal's number.

"Neal Hazard."

"Neal, it's Rhys Maddox."

"Hi. I know I said I'd get back to you earlier this week, but your Albany reference was on vacation. I couldn't get hold of him until today. If you want the job, it's yours."

One, two, three, four, five. Rhys counted so he could come across calmer than he was. "Yes, definitely."

"Good. Can you start Monday?"

"Not a problem."

"I hope the next part isn't, either. We'll be working the Watertown job for the next three weeks. It's about a three-hour drive. The crew has been staying there during the week and coming home on weekends."

Owen and Dylan's fall soccer season was starting already, and he'd promised Owen he'd come to his first game next Tuesday. Then there was that Building Bridges meeting Pastor Connor had told him about. They were all important, but he had to get his priorities straight. He needed a job to regain custody of Owen and Dylan. For now, the job came first. It had to—for his sons.

"If it's not okay, you can start in three weeks," Neal said in response to his hesitation.

"No. I mean, yes, I can start Monday." He had to think long-term, even if Owen would be disappointed, and he'd make Dylan's game tomorrow, his first one. "I didn't ask this at the interview, but do I need my own tools?" Shame washed over him. Gwen had had to sell his.

"The company has tools. You'll probably want to get your own as time goes on."

Rhys smiled at the night sky. *As time goes on.* He liked the sound of that.

"Be at the office at six, Monday morning. We take company trucks."

He patted the side of his pickup. *Another plus.* "I'll be there. Thanks for giving me this opportunity."

"You're qualified. Why wouldn't I?"

Rhys could think of many reasons another man might not. But he simply said, "See you Monday," then hung up.

Rhys pushed off the truck, climbed in and let out a cheer as he headed home, not sure that he'd be getting a whole lot more sleep than if he hadn't called Neal.

Morning's arrival proved him right about the sleep, or lack of it. The two cups of coffee he'd had at home before leaving for Dylan's soccer game had only taken the edge off his sleep-deprivation fog. So he'd stopped at the coffee shop in Schroon Lake for another, which had taken far longer than he'd expected. Now, he was running late for the game.

He approached the field behind the high school and spotted his son. He lifted his hand to raise his arm and get Dylan's attention, so he'd know he was there, but then stopped. Rhys didn't want to embarrass him, or worse, distract Dylan and get him in trouble with his coach.

"Rhys!" Jack Hill beckoned him over to the bleacher where he and Suzi sat.

This morning was supposed to be Dylan's time, so Suzi had arranged for Owen to go to his friend Alex's house.

"Sorry." Rhys lifted his coffee cup. "It took longer than I expected."

"Don't worry," Suzi said. "The game is just starting."

Rhys sat next to Jack. "Did Dylan say anything about me not being here?"

"No, he was fine," Suzi said.

He knew her words were meant to reassure him, but they didn't. Rhys gulped down the rest of his coffee. Thursday afternoon at the lake had gone so well. He'd been looking forward to today and thought Dylan might be, too. He crumpled his empty cup. He was making too big a deal of things.

"Hi, Rhys." A voice he couldn't place at first came from behind him.

He turned. "Hi, Claire." He nodded. "Renee." They were with several other people he assumed were family members.

"Robbie plays on Dylan's team," Claire said.

"Claire, you can socialize later," an older man said. "The game's starting."

"Dad, it's a kids' game, not the World Cup."

"But your bobbing back and forth is distracting," Mr. Delacroix said. "I want to be able to see Robbie."

Claire shook her head and sat back on the bleacher.

Rhys had no intention of socializing with Claire, but he did want to talk privately with Renee about the job and working out of town the next three weeks. It would save him a phone call to CPS on Monday. He'd have to catch her after the game.

He turned his attention to the field. The game was more a comedy of errors than a competition, and he enjoyed every minute of it, cheering Dylan and his team on, along with the Hills and Renee's family behind them. A fleeting thought of Gwen, the only woman he'd ever loved, and what she was missing—what he'd missed—made his joy bittersweet.

Dylan raced over after the game ended. "Suzi, did you see? I kicked the ball three times."

Rhys swallowed his disappointment that his son went to Suzi and not him. He knew he was expecting too much too soon. "That last kick was almost a goal."

"I know." Dylan beamed at him, lifting his

spirits. The boy turned to Jack. "Can we get ice cream on the way home?"

"Sure thing," Jack said. "Your dad can meet us at the ice-cream stand."

Two steps forward. One step back. "I wouldn't miss it. I need to talk with Ms. Delacroix and then I'll be right there."

Dylan nodded and Rhys watched him walk away with the Hills, nearly missing Renee leaving with Claire. He jogged the few steps to catch up with them.

"Renee, I need to talk with you, if you have a minute."

Claire raised an eyebrow. "I'll be at the car."

He rubbed the back of his neck. "About Owen and Dylan."

"I don't…all right," Renee answered.

"Can we sit?" Rhys asked.

She nodded and he led them back to the bleachers they'd just left. He waited until she'd settled on the front bench before sitting.

"I have a job with Hazard Solar starting Monday."

"Congratulations."

Rhys searched her face for an indication that the job was good news for his custody case. "I know. I could have called the office about that on Monday, but there's more. I'll be working in Watertown during the week. I'm going to talk with

Jack and Suzi about weekend visitation. I'm meeting with them at the soft-serve ice-cream stand. They can coordinate with you."

She shook her head. "Didn't your caseworker contact you? My internship with CPS ended yesterday."

His heart sank. He was going to have to start all over with someone else at CPS? Just when he and Renee finally had a working relationship going. While he couldn't say Renee appeared crazy about working with him, she seemed to have been a lot more invested in his boys' welfare than the caseworker. "So I have to contact Ms. Bulmer?"

"I'm afraid so. They don't have another intern lined up yet."

Rhys had hoped to have Owen and Dylan back before CPS shuffled them off from the caseworker to yet another person. He rubbed his palms against his jeans. "How does this go? I call Ms. Bulmer and let her know about the job? Then what?"

Renee turned her body to face him fully. Her gaze softened. "You'll need to provide documentation about the job, and Ms. Bulmer will have to approve any new visitation schedule you and Suzi work out. Be patient with her. All the caseworkers have heavy loads."

Patience wasn't one of his strong points. "But someone will get back to me about visitation?"

"Yes, probably Suzi. Anything else?"

"No." He didn't want to end the conversation. He could ask her what she was doing now that her internship was done. Maybe get that read he wanted on how his job would affect his custody application.

"Okay then, I'm going to get going. Claire's waiting." Renee stood.

The moment was gone. "Right, sure. Thanks for the information."

After Renee left, he rested his elbows on his knees, head in hands. Again, what had he expected? That she'd be excited for him? He felt good about the job and the opportunity it offered him and his boys. That's all that mattered. He was a CPS client, her *former* CPS client, and that was all.

Rhys ignored the hollow feeling in his stomach. Once he had Owen and Dylan back, between caring for them and working, he wouldn't have much time for friendship—with her or anyone else.

Chapter Four

Rhys dropped the wire crimpers into his toolbox and rubbed the back of his neck. He shouldn't feel like he was pulling a fast one, leaving the job in Ticonderoga early. Neal had okayed his working a short day on Thursdays so he could volunteer at the weekly Bridges meetings for the kids at church. The only stipulation was that he make up the time. Working late was no problem while the kids were living with the Hills. He'd worked ten-and eleven-hour days the three weeks in Watertown. And once he had custody, he could rethink the Bridges commitment. No one had said it had to be for life.

A couple of the guys eyed him when he picked up his toolbox. He gripped the handle. The supervisor knew about the arrangement. Rhys hadn't seen any reason to broadcast it.

"See you tomorrow," his supervisor called

down from the roof where they were installing solar panels.

Rhys raised his hand over his head. The others waved back without any signs of begrudging his early departure. He should loosen up, he thought as he cranked the old pickup to life. Having some friends besides Pastor Connor could help when his custody request came before Family Court. He needed all the help he could muster.

A virtual finger poked him in the chest.

I know. I need to get up to speed at trusting You. Give me time. I've trusted only myself for too long.

Going back to the Thursday Bible study group wouldn't hurt, either. Rhys hadn't been there since the group had celebrated Renee's birthday. For the spiritual support, he could tolerate the social aspects he was less fond of.

While he waited to turn onto US Route 74, he checked the dashboard clock. He'd have just enough time to get home to shower and change before he was supposed to meet Pastor Connor and the Bridges program director at the church office. He'd missed the volunteer training meeting when he'd been in Watertown, and today was the first meeting of the new group. Rhys had read the literature Pastor Connor had emailed him and was still uncertain about the group's value, but it would give him another hour a week with Owen and Dylan.

A short way up the road, a dark-haired woman in a subcompact car cut a turn from a side road a little too close in front of him. He pumped the brakes, gritting his teeth against the word that leaped to his tongue and the picture of another dark-haired woman that popped into his head.

The woman in the car wasn't Renee, but the Social Services' worker had been in his thoughts far too often since their talk after the game on Saturday. With her background, Renee could be a good asset at a custody hearing. He grimaced. Except that the jury was still out on whether Renee was a friend or foe.

Rhys had made short work of cleaning up and arrived at the church a couple minutes early.

"Come in. Sit down," Pastor Connor said when Rhys peered around the half-open office door. "Did you have time to look over what I sent?" he asked once Rhys was seated.

"I did."

"What do you think?"

Rhys stretched his legs under the table, drew them back and planted the soles of his boots flat on the floor. "Can I be honest?"

"By all means." The corners of Connor's mouth quirked up.

"It strikes me as outsiders, institutions, meddling in families' lives, especially since the referrals come from the school and CPS."

"But you've agreed to participate."

"Bottom line. I'm not connecting with Dylan, and I can't afford private counseling. My health insurance is good, but there's a higher deductible for specialists. The rent on the house is a stretch until I get better situated."

"Fair enough." Pastor Connor leaned back in his chair. "The Action Coalition isn't only the Building Bridges program. It helps support several other faith-based programs and organizations, like my prison ministry."

Rhys gripped the armrests and narrowed his eyes. He owed Pastor Connor and his prison ministry big time. Was the man looking for payback to get the Bridges thing going here?

"Rather than looking at Building Bridges as an interfering institution, try seeing it as God's hand guiding His followers in helping families in need." Connor grinned and Rhys relaxed.

"I can give that an apprentice's try," Rhys said.

"That's all anyone can ask."

The office door creaked open. "Renee, come in," Pastor Connor said.

Renee. "I thought we were meeting with the director." *Nice job, Maddox.* He accepted the well-deserved frown from Connor. Renee's new job must be as the director of the Christian Action Coalition. That was some step up from a graduate student internship with Social Services. Was it a who-you-know rather than what-you-know position?

Rhys couldn't help losing some confidence in the Coalition and its programs, nor stop the sinking feeling that Renee was acting again as a wall between him and his sons. At least he wouldn't be dealing with her one-on-one after today. From what he'd read, each Building Bridges meeting had a designated facilitator. Pastor Connor had said the director would run the Hazardtown meetings only until someone had been appointed.

"Congratulations on your new job," Rhys said.

Renee gave him a puzzled look. "Thanks."

What had he done now? Rhys was well aware that his upbringing and incarceration hadn't helped anything when it came to the nuances of interpersonal relationships. But what could be wrong with congratulating Renee on such a big career move?

Pastor Connor tapped his finger on the desk. "Let me clear things up. You must have missed the email I sent last night, Rhys."

"I didn't see it." Rhys dropped his gaze to the desktop. He'd said enough about the health insurance and rent. He didn't want to add that generally he checked his email only when he had free

Wi-Fi so he didn't use the limited data he had with his cell phone plan.

"Renee is the facilitator for our meeting and the other elementary school meetings in the county," Pastor Connor continued. "Originally, the director was going to do the Bridges kick-off meetings this week because he wasn't sure when he was going to have Renee on board and up to speed. But he was able to get her into the monthly training session at the national Building Bridges program in Atlanta this week when there was a last-minute cancellation."

Rhys caught Renee's side glance and the tilt of one corner of her mouth. He sank into the hard wooden chair as best he could. She'd picked up that he'd thought she was the Association Director. He'd known she couldn't be. His logic filter had sent out alarms that the rest of his brain and his mouth had ignored. For whatever reason, Renee's presence drained him of what intelligence he had. His blood heated with embarrassment, fueled by the hint of understanding he'd seen—or wanted to see—in her brief smile.

"I just got back this morning," Renee said. "Hazardtown Community is my home church. I wanted to be here to get the program going."

She certainly seemed excited, strikingly more so than he'd seen at any of their CPS meetings. Rhys studied her while her gaze was on Pastor

Connor. Her jeans, long-sleeved red T-shirt that brought out the pink in her cheeks and her dark hair falling down her back in a simple ponytail formed a picture of a more approachable Renee. Someone who lacked the icy veneer that the crisp, business-casual pants and drab shirts she'd worn at CPS had given her. Was this the real Renee? He shook the question from his mind. What did Renee Delacroix's "true" identity matter to him?

"Is there a problem, Rhys?" Pastor Connor asked.

He must have shaken his head. "No."

"Okay, then. We need to get things going. The kids will be here in fifteen minutes. Here's the list of who we expect today." He handed them each a sheet. "Five are here already in the child-care program and the other three, including your boys, Rhys, will be dropped off."

Rhys read the list of six boys and two girls for the names of any friends of Owen's or Dylan's. He didn't see any he knew. Not that he'd expected to. The friends he'd met—his boss's son, Alex, and Renee's nephew—or those Owen had mentioned, came from intact families. His chest tightened. That was the kind of family he'd wanted for his sons, the kind he and Gwen had had before he'd messed up.

"I have a short agenda for today's meeting," Renee said. She pulled a copy for each of the men from a leather bag on the floor between her and Rhys. "I thought I'd leave things open so we can get to know each other."

Rhys laughed as he read the short bullet points. Introductions. A game. Food. "Hey, it sounds good. Playing and eating. I can handle this."

Renee smiled with what looked to him like relief, but he dismissed the thought. She'd never seek his approval.

"I don't have anything else," Pastor Connor said. "Do either of you?"

Renee shook her head.

Rhys had in the ballpark of one hundred questions, but none to be answered here.

"Let's close in prayer, then."

Rhys folded his hands in his lap before he caught the motion of Pastor Connor reaching across the desk to them. He took Connor's hand and reached for Renee's, wishing he'd wiped his against his jeans first. Joining hands in prayer took some getting used to. The Bible study group he'd participated in with Pastor Connor at Dannemora hadn't been as demonstrative as his church congregation's. He bowed his head and blocked out the soft grip of Renee's hand on his, along with memories of what it felt like to hold a woman's hand not in prayer.

"And bless Renee and Rhys in Your service. Amen," Pastor Connor said in closing.

"Amen," he and Renee said, dropping hands.

Renee rose. "We're meeting in my first-and-second-grade Sunday school room. Upstairs."

Rhys stopped halfway between sitting and standing. "You're Dylan's Sunday school teacher?"

"I will be when classes resume in a couple of weeks." She paused by the door while he straightened. "We can go right up. I already put the box of materials for the meeting and the snacks in the room."

"I could have carried them for you." Rhys hated how his voice had the same overeagerness he often heard in Owen's.

"No problem."

Rhys walked beside her in silence down the hall to the stairs, his mind swimming with potential problems. He cleared his throat. "Out of curiosity, did you know that I'd volunteered to work here with the kids?" He forced himself to breathe in and out evenly while he waited for her answer.

"I knew before I came today."

She must not have known, then, when they'd talked on Saturday.

"I think it'll be great for the kids," Renee said.

But not for her, at least according to what he remembered about body language from the one psychology course he'd taken. She held her leather bag like a shield between them.

"You don't have any problem with us, uh, working together, do you?"

"No." She opened the first door at the top of the stairs and led him inside. "Why should I?"

Right, why should you?

Renee tucked the doorstop under the door as she waited for his answer—if he was going to answer at all. She understood how he might have seen her as an adversary in her position at CPS. But he didn't need to carry it over to the Bridges program. They were both here for the kids.

"Hi, Miss Renee." A little girl with long blond braids skipped past her into the room. "Mrs. Hill let me walk upstairs by myself, since this is my Sunday school room."

"Hi, Emma. You're right on time to help us set up." Now that Emma was in the room, Renee let her question to Rhys drop, even though she would have liked to hear his answer. Any insight into the man would help them work together better, which could benefit both them and the kids.

The little girl looked at Rhys. "Who's he?"

"He's my helper, Mr. Ma—"

Rhys frowned, and Renee remembered him asking her to use his first name at the home visit she'd supervised at the Hills' house.

"Mr. Rhys." She corrected herself.

"Hi, Emma," he said.

His face broke into a welcoming smile that charmed Emma. It also calmed some of the apprehension Renee had had about Rhys working with her and the children, while filling her with a wistful emptiness. *Okay*, the rational professional in her said. *So he never smiles that way at you. Why should he?*

Or maybe the bigger question was why did part of her want him to?

Emma faced off with him, hands on her hips. "Are you Miss Renee's boyfriend?"

"Ah, n-no," he sputtered.

The pink that tinged his sharp cheekbones shrunk the hollowness inside Renee. Rhys did have human emotions that extended beyond his sons. *But not for you.*

"I was just asking," Emma said. "Because my daddy has a girlfriend. That's why Mommy says I have to come to this club, to adapt."

Renee stifled the giggle Rhys's raised eyebrow brought to her lips. "Emma's parents are divorced, and her father is marrying again."

"I see." Rhys's lips twitched as he schooled his face into a serious look.

"So, if you're not Miss Renee's boyfriend, why are you here?"

"To help her with the boys."

"Boys can be such a problem." Emma continued to scrutinize Rhys. "Do you have kids?"

"I do. I have two boys."

"Oh, no," Emma said, turning her head to the open doorway where Owen and Dylan stood with Suzi Hill behind them, waving to Renee.

"It's Dylan Maddox." The little girl turned her gaze to Renee. "He's going to be here?"

Rhys's jaw tightened at Emma's tone as Renee's mind scrambled for a fast way to defuse the tension.

"Dylan's in my grade and thinks he's so smart because he can read chapter books."

Rhys pulled out his kid smile again, the one that had an irritating habit of going straight to Renee's heart.

"I'm Dylan and Owen's dad."

The pride in his voice registered with Renee, if not with Emma, who turned her head from father to son and back as if she couldn't fathom the connection.

"Hi, Dad," Owen said, moving toward Rhys with Dylan trailing behind.

"Hey, Owen, Dylan."

Emma nodded. "That's why you're here. You're building your family, too."

Rhys shrugged and shuffled his foot. "Something like that."

"Everybody come in and sit down so we can get started," Renee said, motioning to Karen Hill, Suzi's mother-in-law and one of the teachers at the child-care center, and the four boys she was herding in from the hall. A preschool-age girl clung to Karen's hand as if the woman was her lifeline.

"Grandma Hill." Dylan ran toward the door and flung his arms around the woman's waist.

Rhys winced. While Renee had given plenty of thought to working with Rhys, she hadn't thought about Karen being here and the dynamics between Rhys's boys and him and Karen. She'd talk with Karen and Pastor Connor before the next meeting.

"This is Melody," Karen said, extricating herself from Dylan's hug and moving toward the little girl in front of her. "She's four and joined our pre-K class this week."

Renee squatted to Melody's level and the girl stuck her thumb in her mouth. "I'm Miss Renee. Do you want to come and sit next to me? We're going to play a game and have brownies and a drink for snack."

Melody nodded, grasped Renee's hand— thumb still firmly in her mouth—and walked with her to the table. Melody was the only one of the kids she didn't already know from helping with Sunday school last school year.

"Come on, guys, Emma. We need to sit down, too," Rhys said. The boys jostled each other to get to the table first.

"Can you get the journals from the other table?" Renee asked him as she pulled out a chair for Melody and sat next to her.

"I'll save you a place, Dad," Owen said, indicating the seat beside him at the opposite end of the table.

"Me, too," Emma echoed, sitting on the other side and throwing her arm across his.

It looked like Rhys had made himself a friend, although Renee imagined he'd prefer to have Dylan sitting there, rather than next to her, where he'd chosen to sit.

"Dylan, would you please help by bringing me half of the books?" she asked.

"I guess." He pushed back from the table and went to his father.

Renee caught nearly identical unreadable expressions on father and son's faces as Rhys gave Dylan half of the journals to carry. Rhys placed the remainder on the table in front of him.

Renee breathed deeply. "Okay, most of you know who I am, Miss Renee, and I know you. But not everyone knows each other. To all get to know everyone better, we're going to go around the table and introduce ourselves by answering three questions. Your name, your grade and what you want to do when you grow up. I'll start and pass the books I have for you to Dylan. He'll take one, answer the question and pass the pile to the next person."

"But, Miss Renee," Emma said, "you and Mr. Rhys are already grown up."

"Don't worry. I have that covered. My name is Miss Renee, and when I was in fifth grade, I collected fossils and wanted to be a paleontologist."

"What are you now?" one of the boys asked as she placed the pile of books in front of Dylan.

It was the same question she'd been asking herself lately. The tableful of children eyed her, waiting.

"I was a missionary in Haiti. Now I'm a group leader for the Building Bridges program."

"And a Sunday school teacher," Emma said.

"Yes, Emma." She might have to rein in Emma's enthusiasm to give the other kids the opportunity to participate. "Dylan, you're up."

He lifted the top book from the pile and held it upright in front of him. "My name is Dylan Maddox, and I'm going into first grade. When I grow up, I want to drive a tow truck like Mr. Hill." He pushed the pile of books at the boy next to him.

Renee bit her lip. Was Rhys's son purposely goading him? As a family, they might have a larger gap to close than she—and she suspected Rhys, also—had thought they had.

The two boys seated between Dylan and Owen shared their information, then Owen took the remaining books. "I'm Owen Maddox, Dylan's brother. I'm going into fourth grade and I'm going to be a racecar driver and then a racecar designer when I grow up. Your turn, Dad."

"I'm Rhys Maddox. You can call me Mr. Rhys."

"Not Daddy?" Dylan blurted.

"No, stu—"

Rhys stopped Owen with a dark look. "Dylan, you can call me Daddy."

Melody pulled her thumb out of her mouth. "Can I call you Daddy? My daddy went away."

Rhys looked at Renee with the desperation of a drowning man.

She smoothed Melody's curls back from her face, her heart cracking. From the background the Action Coalition had provided about the little girl, she knew her mother's National Guard unit had been deployed overseas and that Melody was staying with a grandmother she barely knew. A situation that wasn't a lot different from Dylan and Rhys's. "I think you should call him Mr. Rhys like I do."

The thumb went back into her mouth and the crack in Renee's heart widened.

"I can call him Mr. Rhys, too," Dylan offered.

Renee answered Rhys's pained stare with a forced smile. She patted Dylan's hand. "That's very nice of you, Dylan. It's okay for you and

Owen to call your father 'Dad.' The rest of us will call him Mr. Rhys."

"Okay."

Renee crossed her hands in front of her and looked down the table to Rhys. "Please, finish your introduction," she said in her best Sunday-school-teacher voice.

He gave her his first true smile. "As Miss Renee said, I'm Mr. Rhys, and I install solar panels on roofs and do electric wiring. When I was in school, I wanted to be a gold medalist in swimming."

Renee replayed the afternoon they'd met at the lake, including him making short work of cutting out to the middle of the lake. She'd wondered whether he'd swum competitively.

The next two boys introduced themselves and the second one passed the last journal to Melody. The little girl looked up at Renee, the uncertainty in her big blue eyes tugging at Renee's heartstrings and causing her stomach to sink. It was only halfway through her first Bridges meeting and she was already too invested in the kids.

"Go ahead, sweetie."

"I'm Melody," she said in a voice barely above a whisper. "I just started pre-K. And I *don't* want to be a soldier when I grow up."

Renee cleared her throat. "Thank you, Melody, everyone. Now if you'll open the journals we passed around, you'll find a letter to give to your parent." She glanced sideways at Melody. "Or grandparent. It explains how we're going to use the journals and asks for some ideas for things we can do as families. We'll talk about that at our meeting next week."

Dylan tugged at her shirtsleeve. "Doesn't Daddy already know what we're doing with the books?"

Rhys's nod told her Pastor Connor must have filled him in. "Yes, he knows."

"So do we give it to the Hills?"

She stopped herself from glancing at Rhys again. This was her meeting. She didn't need to check with Rhys. Until CPS okayed unsupervised visitation, the Hills would be involved in any family outings. "Yes, give the note to Mrs. Hill. Now, everyone write his or her name in your journal while Mr. Rhys and I get the snacks. There are pencils in the holder in the middle of the table."

As if she'd lowered a flag to signal the start of a race, the older boys lunged for the holder. But Rhys was faster. He held it up. "We'll pass the pencils around."

Renee smiled her thanks. She could see advantages to having him at the meetings. As she got up, Melody sniffed. She sat, journal open, pencil gripped in her little hand.

"I don't know how to write my name."

Serge, one of the older boys, snickered.

"Serge and I can get the snack." Rhys's voice made it clear he wasn't making a suggestion. He directed the boy to the other table.

Renee wet her lips. Building Bridges' policy on when and how to discipline had been part of the meeting Rhys had missed. She'd listen carefully to what Rhys said to Serge.

She took Melody's hand in hers and wrote her name. "Thanks, Miss Renee." Melody gave her a shy smile. "You're pretty and smell nice, like my mommy when she's not being a soldier."

"Thank you." Renee sensed Rhys behind her and turned. Before he handed her the plate of brownies, something flashed in his eyes that for a second melted the coldness they usually held.

Had he heard Melody? She began to melt, too.

"Serge will pass out the napkins, and I'll pour the drinks," he said, the look gone, as if it had never been there.

She took a brownie and placed one on a napkin for Melody before giving the plate to Dylan. What had she been thinking? The only softness she'd seen in Rhys was for his sons. Had Melody captivated him as much as the little girl had captivated her? If so, the firmness he'd showed with Serge—directing him to do something constructive without making a big deal about his rude behavior—along with how much he cared for the kids, could make Rhys the asset to the program Pastor Connor thought he'd be.

She took in the group, Rhys included, who were all wolfing down the snack. She'd have to institute the blessing at the next meeting.

Yes. She could handle working with Rhys. All she needed to do was to maintain some professional distance between them.

"Tough crowd," Rhys said fifteen minutes later after the last of the kids had been picked up. The hour had been different from anything he'd experienced before.

"Can't argue with that." Renee scooped up the two journals left on the table. "I half expected Emma to ask her mother if she could bring you home with her."

"She's a pistol." Rhys repositioned one of the chairs at the table. "If only Dylan were half as attached to me."

"It'll come with time," Renee said in a tone Rhys had dubbed her social-worker voice, the voice she'd used at CPS when he'd asked her a question she couldn't answer directly.

A dull weight settled in his chest. Their camaraderie from the meeting was over and Renee was retreating behind the barrier of her professional persona.

"Do you have a minute, or do you need to get

home?" Renee asked, straightening the edges of the two books on the table.

"I have time. There's nothing really to get home to." He nudged the chair an inch farther under the table. *That sounded pitiful.*

Renee stepped toward him and he pulled out the chair for her.

"Thanks." She slid into it.

He folded himself into the one next to it and breathed in and out to prepare for what he expected to be constructive criticism. A light floral scent stopped him mid-exhale. Little Melody had been right. Miss Renee did smell nice. He tilted his chair back, away from her, to give himself some much-needed space.

"I want to talk about Serge," she said.

Rhys froze. *Here it comes.*

"It wasn't in the background material we got, but he didn't want to be in the group. His mother told me. She's a friend of my older sister's."

"Claire?"

Renee's eyes darkened to almost black. "No. My oldest sister, Andie." She waved her hand. "Anyway. You handled him well. You were firm and caring."

"I'll take that as a real compliment coming from a pro like you."

Renee tipped her head to the side. If he'd sounded sarcastic or mocking, he hadn't meant it that way. *You can do this, Maddox. Don't be intimidated. We're all equal in God's eyes.* He looked her full in the face.

"We're going to make you a pro, too." Renee's words sounded forced.

The only thing he was considering making at the moment was a quick getaway.

"You missed the Bridges' behavior management training and strategies on discipline given at the volunteer orientation meeting."

Rhys crossed his arms at his chest. He hadn't intentionally skipped it; his job had been priority one.

"You should have that training. It will help you when you have Owen and Dylan." Renee bit her lip as if she'd said too much.

Did she know something he didn't? She was close friends with Suzi and still had her contacts at CPS.

Rhys lassoed in the buoyancy bubbling up inside him. More likely, the training would be during the workday again, and she was expecting resistance. Might as well clear the air. "I can't take off work. Neal's been more than accommodating with my leaving early on Thursdays for this."

"I understand. We can do it in the evenings."

Rhys uncrossed his arms. "You and me?"

Renee's hand fluttered above the table before

she pushed a nonexistent lock of hair behind her ear. "Yes. I mean, another facilitator and I are offering the training during evenings at the Action Coalition office in Elizabethtown."

"Okay. Do you have the information about it?"

"I'll email you the details. You can follow up online or by phone."

"I'll be on the lookout for it." The training certainly couldn't hurt. His role models for caring discipline had been few and far between.

"Good, that's it." Renee stood and gave him a smile that glued him to his seat.

He pushed away from the table. Two minutes ago, he'd been ready to bolt. No other woman had ever taken him on these choppy seas Renee continually had him navigating. Gwen certainly hadn't. She'd been the calm center in his life. He twisted his mouth in confusion. Why was he thinking of Renee in comparison with Gwen?

"Did you have another question?" Renee asked.

He mentally grasped for something to cover his disorientation. "Are you going to the Twenty-/Thirtysomethings meeting tonight?"

"Didn't you get the email?"

"I didn't see it." Rhys stood, gripping the chair back as if he needed the support. Because he hadn't checked. He really needed to make an effort to do that more regularly when he had Wi-Fi access.

"Tonight is the championship race for the kids who participated in the summer session of Jared Donnelly's motocross school. Half of the group's members are either volunteering or have kids participating, and most of the others wanted to go. Jared and a couple of his former racing circuit buddies are going to do an exhibition. So Pastor Connor decided to cancel. His and Jared's little sister is racing."

"The one who's Owen age?" Motocross seemed more like something for teenagers.

"Yep, Hope. Jared runs a racing program for kids, particularly at-risk kids. It's based on tenets similar to those of the Big Brothers Big Sisters organization." Her face lit up. "I can send you information on that, too, if you think Owen or Dylan would be interested."

He jammed his hands into the front pockets of his jeans. His sons weren't "at risk." He was making sure of that. They certainly didn't need another big brother/father figure to confuse them. They'd had Jack Hill for the past few months, and now they had him. And he didn't need Renee making him and his boys her pet project.

"Jared has a foundation that funds the program, and the Christian Action Committee helps, so it costs parents next to nothing."

He curled his fingers. Had she just assumed he couldn't afford the motocross school or had he become that easy to read? In his former life, his poker face had been his trademark asset. He pulled his hands from his pockets and flexed them. He had a good job now. Give him a month and he'd be able to upgrade his cell service and pay for motocross school if either of his boys was interested—and anything else they wanted or needed. He didn't need charity.

Renee glanced at the clock on the wall. "Walk out with me. We finished later than I'd expected and I need to meet Claire at home." Renee added, "Maybe get something to eat before we go to the race." She flicked off the lights and headed out the door, seemingly sure he'd follow.

Her uncharacteristic friendliness halted Rhys's step.

"You should come."

He caught up with her, suppressing a lifelong desire to belong.

"I mean, meet us at the track, not for dinner." Renee turned toward the door he'd closed behind them and locked it.

He knew what she'd meant, but that didn't stop his disappointment. He had to stop picking up the mixed signals he knew Renee *couldn't* be sending—they were only driving him crazy.

Renee checked the door. "It's church policy to lock rooms that aren't in use."

He nodded. She'd felt the need to reassure him

she wasn't locking it against him? Apparently he'd lost his alligator hide, along with his poker face, at least when it came to her. "I'll think about that, meeting the group."

"Do that. It'll be fun."

He had been thinking he could use some spiritual support earlier. But he'd been envisioning something more Bible-based.

Renee's phone rang. "It's my grandmother. I should take it."

"Sure." Rhys left her to her call. What he should be thinking about was why he was considering going to the race. Why he'd want to walk voluntarily into the storm that any contact with Renee brought down on his emotions.

Chapter Five

A half hour later Renee strode up the side-walk to her apartment, Rhys intruding on her thoughts. They'd worked well together with the kids. Things hadn't gone as well once the kids had left, though. He didn't intimidate her as he had when they'd first met at CPS, but he had a restlessness about him that put her on edge.

The heavy wooden door to the triplex stuck as it often did in hot, humid weather. Before school started, someone needed to clue Rhys in that the district used emails and texts to notify parents about school events and alert them to winter school delays and closings. She lifted her damp hair from her neck, yanked the door open and closed it with a bang. That someone wasn't her. Her obligations to Rhys started and ended with the Bridges meetings and family events. Between the time her boss had told her Rhys would be working with the group and the meeting today, she'd mentally resolved any personal problems she might have had with him being her group volunteer. Renee blew a puff of air that ruffled her bangs. Next time she saw Suzi, she'd suggest Suzi talk with Rhys about email and the school.

"Who won, you or the door? I heard the bang and then you stomping up the stairs," Claire greeted her.

"I did not. Stomp, that is."

"Yes, you did."

"Okay, I did."

"Want to tell me about it? The kids give you trouble?"

Renee threw herself into the closest chair. "No, the kids were as good as I expected them to be. There's the sweetest little four-year-old, Melody, who's new to The Kids Place. She's staying with her grandmother while her mother is deployed with her National Guard unit. I couldn't place who her grandmother is. I need to ask Karen or Pastor Connor. And you wouldn't—or maybe you would—believe how Emma Koch attached herself to Rhys. I thought she'd ask her mother if she could take Rhys home with her."

"So that's your problem—your helper." Claire smirked.

Renee rubbed her temples. It was beyond her comprehension why she'd pressed him to come to the race tonight. Her long day must have taken more out of her than she'd thought.

"Hey, you're not going to claim a headache and bail on me, are you? Leave me all alone with Andie?" Claire gave an exaggerated shudder.

"I thought your friend Nick was going to meet us there."

"Right, I don't want to be alone with Nick and our big sister. Andie is worse than Mom when it comes to male friends. You'd think I was one of her kids, by how she treats me."

"Speaking of which, are the kids coming with Andie?"

"No, Robbie wanted to stay home. The twins are going to watch him while their father does the evening milking. Apparently the twins aren't on Andie's A-list this week, and she needs a girls' night out."

"Good, I'm not up for the cloud of fifteen-year-old drama that hangs over Aimee and Amelia," Renee said.

"Have you eaten?" Claire asked.

"No, I thought we were going to get something on the way."

Claire shrugged. "I had a sandwich. Remember, we need to swing by and pick up Andie."

"And we'll never hear the end of it if we're late. I'll get something at the racetrack. But I want to change before we go." Renee eyed Claire's waist-hugging cotton dress with its flared skirt. "A dress?"

"Why not? The weather is stifling and it's cool." Claire twirled around. "Besides, the last time I wore it, Nick complimented me."

Renee patted herself on the back for not rolling her eyes. "I'll be quick." She mentally inventoried what she might have clean.

"And take it easy on Andie," Claire said. "With the kids, her classes, her job at the day-care center and helping Rob on the farm, she doesn't get much time for herself." Claire smoothed her skirt. "The last being one of the reasons you'll never see me married to a dairy farmer."

"I'll be right back," Renee said, laughing to herself as she climbed the stairs. She'd heard that pronouncement from Claire too many times to count. But at least Claire knew what she wanted—or didn't want—in a man. After her disastrous romance in Haiti, reading too much into her relationship with a medic who'd failed to share that he'd had a fiancée stateside, Renee was uncertain whether she had the judgment to pick a good man from a bad one.

A picture of Rhys earlier today with his too often brooding eyes crinkling with laughter at some outrageous thing Emma had said flashed in Renee's mind, juxtaposed over a picture of him at his wife's funeral last spring with leg irons, flanked by two correctional officers, falling to his knees in grief. Her heart squeezed. She shook off the vision and transferred her thoughts to clothes. Her gaze moved to her open closet and her turquoise tie-dyed handkerchief dress. Rhys had never seen her in a dress. She walked over and touched the soft fabric.

"You almost ready?" Claire called up the stairs.

"Almost." Renee dropped the fabric, spun back around to the dresser and pulled out a pair of cotton shorts and a plain pink T-shirt. With the dry weather they'd had this month, the track grounds would be dusty, so she put on her athletic shoes. She pulled her hair back into a high ponytail and reached for her mascara before pausing. Who did she need to put makeup on for? *Certainly not Rhys*, she answered herself as she bounded down the stairs.

Granted, he was attractive in that dangerous way that appealed to some women. That had never been her type. Besides, he was an ex-convict. They had nothing in common except his volunteering with Building Bridges, which he'd been half coerced into. She stopped and checked her appearance in the gilt-framed mirror at the bottom of the stairs. So why did she keep thinking about him?

Because, despite all that, she was drawn to him. Chalk it up to her flawed judgment when it came to men. Renee moistened her lips and grabbed her bag from where she'd dropped it earlier.

A little lip gloss couldn't hurt.

The smell of gas and the roar of motors hit them when Renee and her sisters hopped out of Claire's car in the racetrack parking lot forty-five minutes later. Renee's empty stomach lurched at the fumes. Her first stop would be the refreshment stand. A nice juicy cheeseburger should hit the spot.

"I'm going to go get something to eat. How about you guys?"

"You should have eaten at home," Andie said. "The stuff here will be greasy and overpriced."

"And benefit the race program," Renee said. Like Claire, she hated when Andie treated her as if she was one of her kids. Only it was worse for her, with the eldest/youngest dynamic thrown in.

"I want to see if Nick is here yet." Claire glanced around the parking lot. "I texted him that we're here, but you know how cell reception can be. Would you keep a lookout for his car on your way? He said he'd wait for us in the parking lot."

"Sure thing." Renee headed toward the concession stand, looking for Nick's car and another familiar pickup.

By the time she reached the archway, she

hadn't seen either vehicle. For Claire's sake, she hoped Nick hadn't bowed out at the last minute. It wouldn't be the first time. And for her own sake, her nerves could live without Rhys showing. As she approached the refreshment stand, the aroma of beef grilling overtook the petroleum fumes. Renee pressed her hand to her stomach as it growled in anticipation.

"I'll have a cheeseburger, fries, Sprite and fried dough."

"Confectionary sugar on the fried dough?" the woman behind the counter asked.

"Definitely." Junk food, friends and a little fun and excitement. It sounded like just the prescription she needed for the stress of her busy week of training and work.

Kari Koch was a full-size version of her daughter Emma. She had an opinion on everything and was every bit as clingy. She'd just touched Rhys's arm to make a point—for probably the third time. He eyed the dwindling empty spots farther down the bleacher row. It would be rude to get up and move.

He'd gotten to the track early and had sat in the section where Connor had told him the Twenty-/Thirtysomethings group would be sitting. A few minutes later Kari and another woman had plopped down beside him. She'd introduced them and then said he must be the new member of the group they'd heard about. Although she hadn't been at the meeting he'd attended—he would have remembered—and he couldn't recall seeing her at church, from the way Kari was leaning into him now, you'd think they were old friends. An itch like a line of ants crawled up his spine.

Rhys leaned into the space beside him, regretting his decision not to join Claire Delacroix when he'd arrived. He'd spotted her and a woman who looked so much like her and Renee that she had to be another sister, or at least a cousin, at the other end of the bleachers. Pastor Connor and most of the other people he knew from church were sitting with Claire now. The noise of the crowd blocked out every other word of Kari's chatter.

Better yet, I should have stayed home.

He surveyed the people below and the kids warming up on the track sidelines before glancing past Kari to the woman on her other side. Mandy? Marcy? He couldn't recall her name, but Kari had introduced her as a friend. She didn't appear to have any problem with Kari focusing all of her attention on him. Rhys looked away before the woman or Kari caught his glance.

"Renee, up here," he called, relief filling him when he spotted her juggling a drink and a cardboard tray of food. He patted the empty space next to him on the bleacher bench as if he'd been waiting for her. The way she stopped dead and the strained look on her face when she recognized him didn't do anything for his spur-of-the-moment plan to detach himself from Kari.

Renee's gaze darted to her sisters, but she continued up the aisle toward him. "Hi, Kari." Her smile didn't reach her eyes, but he doubted Kari noticed, focused as she was on him. "Rhys."

"Hi. I saved you a seat," Rhys said.

When Renee made no move toward the space, the ants marched back down his spine. He fidgeted on the bench. How long did a motocross competition last?

"Oh, I thought I'd told you. Claire is saving us seats."

He could have jumped up and hugged her, except, even with his sketchy social skills, he knew that would be inappropriate and would make Renee at least as uncomfortable as Kari was making him.

"Sorry." He stood and edged by Kari, doing his best not to brush her knees. "Previous commitment." He didn't care if he sounded stiff. "It was nice meeting you."

"I'm sure we'll see each other around." Kari's voice flattened a notch.

"You're a sanity saver," he said when they were out of Kari's earshot.

"You do owe me one for that."

Was that a gloating glimmer in Renee's eyes? As for owing her, he added it to his other debts.

A microphone crackled below. "Testing. Testing."

"The races are going to start soon," Renee said.

"I can carry the food or drink so we can hustle."

She handed her drink to him and picked up her pace. "Now we're even."

Not really, but he'd accept it. He disliked being beholden to anyone.

"Renee, we were afraid you'd gotten lost," Claire called when they got within sight of the church group. "Hi, Rhys."

"Hey, everyone." Rhys started toward an empty space on the other side of Pastor Connor and his pregnant wife, Natalie, away from the other Delacroix sisters.

Smiling, Connor and Natalie moved into that space, leaving room for two between Natalie and Claire. They couldn't be thinking of him and Renee as a couple. He gritted his teeth. Connor *had* been kind of pushy about Owen and Dylan being in the Bridges program and him helping Renee at the meetings and events.

No. The only one thinking like that was him. Rhys gathered his errant wits. And the only team efforts he wanted were those that would help him get custody of his sons.

"Come on." Renee motioned with her food tray.

"Sit down," someone shouted from higher up in the stands.

Renee grabbed his elbow and pulled him to the bleacher where her family was sitting. She took the spot next to Natalie and he sat next to her. Engines roared below, sending a burst of adrenaline through him. It had to be the engines.

"Thanks. You want to try some of my fried dough?" Renee tore off a piece.

As if in answer, his stomach grumbled—but he wasn't hungry. He'd already eaten.

"Go ahead," the unidentified Delacroix to his left said. "Her eyes are always larger than her stomach."

Renee frowned.

"No thanks," he said, as the sweet, greasy aroma of her food mixed with the bikes' exhaust fumes.

"Anyone else?" Renee asked.

Natalie accepted some. "I'm eating for two, you know."

His stomach settled.

"I'm Andie Bissette," the woman on his left introduced herself. "Renee's sister."

Ah, she must be the oldest sister. "Rhys Maddox."

"I know." She nodded. "You're…" He braced himself for whatever she might say. "Dylan's father. He's one of my son Robbie's friends."

Rhys relaxed. "Yes, I met Robbie at the lake." Did her eyes narrow? "A few weeks ago, Renee and Claire were there with him and Dylan." *Right, obviously the little boy wouldn't have been there by himself.*

"Renee's birthday. I'd suggested a movie in Ticonderoga."

Renee leaned toward him. "But the boys wanted to go swimming, and Claire and I really are old enough to watch Robbie swim."

"Andie can be a little overprotective sometimes," Claire added.

Renee made a choking sound.

He touched her arm. "Are you okay?"

Renee cleared her throat. "Fine." She pulled her elbow closer in, and he dropped his hand to his lap.

Andie waved her sisters off. "They don't know what it's like to be a parent. You want to keep your kids safe and secure. Right?"

What could he say? He hadn't kept Owen, Dylan or Gwen safe.

Andie went on. "Did you know that some of the kids racing are almost as young as Robbie and Dylan?"

"No, I didn't." Rhys hadn't felt this much in the hot seat since his trial.

"Yes, the youngest are eight years old! I didn't bring Robbie because I didn't want him getting any ideas. I see you didn't bring Dylan and his brother, either." Andie nodded in agreement with herself.

He squirmed on the unforgiving bench. He didn't want to get into the fact that he hadn't had a choice.

"Andie. Dylan and Owen are going on vacation with the Hills tomorrow. Suzi and Jack want to get an early start," Renee reminded her.

"Oh, I forgot," Andie said.

Rhys focused on not clenching his fists and the boys and girls lining up their bikes at the starting line. Had Andie forgotten that the Hills were going on vacation, or was she purposely drawing attention to the fact that he didn't have much of a say in what his sons did or where they went?

Renee touched his arm to get his attention, the same way Kari had kept doing. But Renee's touch didn't irritate him. She motioned with her index finger for him to lean closer. "We usually change the subject when Andie goes off on one of her supermom tangents."

"I'll remember that." What Andie had said didn't strike him as out of line. But what did he know about parenting? Gwen had been the responsible one with Owen and Dylan. He'd just played with his little guys.

"That's what friends are for," Renee said.

By the time Rhys recovered from the wrecking ball smashing his insides, Renee was talking with Natalie. He and Renee were friends?

Rhys ran his hand through his hair. This feeling that he was walking a tightrope without a net was why he stuck to his own business and didn't socialize. The sooner he had Owen and Dylan with him and could concentrate on the three of them as a family, the better.

"Is everyone ready for some excitement?" Jared Donnelly asked the people in the stands from the announcer's platform below.

"Yes!" Renee shouted back with the crowd.

"We're going to start with the eight-to-ten-year-old division." Jared explained what the kids had learned this summer and introduced the racers as he waited for two volunteers to check the kids' bikes and helmet straps.

"Keep an eye on number nine," Pastor Connor said.

"That's Pastor Connor and Jared's little sister, Hope." Renee moved forward in her seat to get a better view of the mini course for the youngest competitors.

She turned her head toward Rhys when he didn't say anything and visually traced his craggy profile from the long, inky eyelashes down his aquiline nose and over his firm lips to his square chin. He seemed to have pulled into himself, as she'd seen him do at CPS when she'd said something he didn't agree with, or when she couldn't directly answer a question.

"Hmm?" he asked when he realized she'd spoken to him.

"Number nine is Pastor Connor's sister."

"The one who's in Owen's class?" Rhys continued to look out over the track. "Owen was so jazzed about racing his car in the Pinewood Derby. He'd like to be here."

"You did know that Jack and Suzi are taking Owen and Dylan with them to visit Boston?"

In a flash, Rhys switched his attention to her. "Yeah. I talked with my lawyer and Suzi about the possibility of them staying with me or Karen Hill. Suzi and Jack are celebrating their tenth wedding anniversary."

Renee didn't have to ask how that went, since

as far as she knew, Rhys's visits with Owen and Dylan were still CPS supervised.

"Ours—Gwen and mine—was this spring, before…"

The pain in his words slashed at her heart.

Rhys cleared his throat. "Do you know if any of Owen's friends race?"

Renee grabbed onto the change of subject. "Not surprisingly, Jared's three kids do. Ariana may be in Owen's class, or a year behind. He'd know her from Sunday school. Ryan Hazard races. He's Alex's cousin and the same age. None of Neal's three kids do. They're more into fishing."

Rhys lifted his eyebrow and the corners of his lips turned up.

"What?" Renee asked.

"Just wondering. Do you know all the kids at Schroon Lake Central?"

Renee laughed. "All the ones whose families belong to Hazardtown Community Church, and a lot more. Kids of my friends and my sisters' and brothers' friends. It's no great feat. The whole school only has two hundred some students."

"I had more than that in my graduating class." His eyes lost the hint of humor she'd seen in them a moment ago. "My would-be graduating class."

The loss of warmth in his eyes drew attention to the cooling night air. Renee hugged herself.

"Cold?" he asked.

She unfolded her arms. "For a second. Things should warm up once the races start." Renee looked to the track to see what the delay was. A volunteer was adjusting something on one of the kids' motorcycles. "I should warn you that I was a cheerleader all four years of high school."

He drew his mouth into a thin line.

Renee studied her nails. Why was she babbling about high school, of all things?

"Looks like we're ready," Jared announced. "As I said, this racing class will do two laps of the modified track."

The starting gate dropped and number nine burst into an instant lead.

"Go, Hope!" Renee shouted, feeling Rhys's gaze on her. "Hey, I warned you." She shot to her feet to see the first jump better.

"So you did." Rhys stood, and when Hope cleared the first jump, he called, "Go, Hope!"

Renee looked over her shoulder.

He grinned. "The only two friends Owen has mentioned to me are Alex and Hope. I think he may have a little thing for her." Rhys wiggled his eyebrows.

Renee twisted the silver cross she wore on a chain around her neck. Like she was feeling a little thing for Owen's father? She dropped the cross. No, the only thing she felt was unsettled every time Rhys did something warm that showed he had emotions—like teasing about Owen's possible crush.

"Owen will have to get in line on that one. Hope can outrace, outrun and outplay most of the boys in her grade. They both envy and like her for her sportsmanship. She also won the third-grade math award last year, and I hear she's never liked dolls."

Rhys's whistle above the noise of the crowd made her smile. "Quite a woman."

His gaze caught and held hers until she refocused on Hope approaching the second jump. Had anyone around her heard that? Renee shifted her weight on the hard wood. They wouldn't think he'd meant her? Renee dismissed it when Hope hit the jump off to the right and her bike wobbled on the landing. Renee and the other spectators gasped.

"See," Andie said. "That's what I meant." She covered her eyes. "I can't see her fall."

"She didn't." Rhys tapped Andie's shoulder when Hope righted the bike and sped around the turn back to the starting line as if nothing had happened.

"Thanks." Andie dropped her hands. "But you see what I mean. Too nerve-racking for me to let Robbie even think about doing that."

"Yes, yes, I do," Rhys said.

Facing straight ahead as though concentrating

on the race, Renee glanced sideways. Who was this sociable Rhys Maddox who could tease about his son's crush and reassure her sister?

Renee sat, leaving Rhys plenty of room on the bench. She looked down to the aisle and thought about going to get another soft drink, even though she didn't actually want one, and sitting on the end when she returned. But knowing her sisters, it would only raise questions if she asked Natalie and Connor to scoot down to make room.

Several races later, during which Renee had kept her comments to Rhys few and short, Rhys leaned toward her and asked, "Want another drink? I'm going to go get one."

"No, thank you." Her answer sounded so prissy, even to her, that she wasn't surprised when Rhys jerked straight back in his seat.

He stood. "Anyone want something from the refreshment stand?"

"I could use a drink," Natalie and Andie both said, Andie frowning at Renee.

"I could use some food, too," Pastor Connor said. "I'll come with you." They collected orders and money.

Once the guys were gone, Renee braced herself for the big-sister lecture Andie's sour expression foretold. But on what? Being too polite? "I'm going to hit the ladies' room," she said before

Andie could start in. She didn't wait to see if any of her sisters wanted to come with her.

When she returned, Rhys was sitting with Pastor Connor. They rose and let her by to her seat next to Natalie.

"You okay?" Natalie asked.

"Sure. Why?"

Natalie motioned with her eyes toward Rhys.

"Yeah, I'm fine," Renee said.

"I thought maybe he'd said something to you. You got quiet after the first race."

"Oh, no." Renee waved her off. "I was just paying careful attention. I feel closer to Hope than the other kids, her being family and all."

Natalie seemed to accept her answer, although she wasn't so sure Claire and Andie would have. Renee and Natalie were nearest in age and had been very close growing up, until Natalie had gone away to college. Now, Renee was closer to Claire, and Andie had always played the big-sister role in all of their lives, whether they wanted her to or not.

Jared announced the next class of racers and Renee made a point of loudly cheering for all the kids she knew. An hour later, he wrapped up the night.

"I want to thank Ross Turrow and Keenan Bliss for taking time out of their race schedule to work with the kids and show us their stuff."

He nodded at his former racing team friends and waited for the applause to die down. "I also want to thank all of the volunteers, especially my bro Connor for the spiritual guidance he's provided the program, and my wife, Becca, for understanding the time commitment this past week has required. But most of all, I'd like a big hand for all of the racers who completed the program this summer."

Along with everyone else in the group, Renee rose and gave the kids a standing ovation. As she sat, she felt her bag slip off her seat and leaned down to retrieve it before it fell through the space between the benches. Someone said, "See everyone Sunday." When she lifted her head, Rhys was already gone, mixing in with the crowd working its way down the bleachers.

"So what's with you and Tall, Dark and Intriguing?" Claire asked after they'd said goodbye to her friend Nick at his car.

"Nothing. I told you, Pastor Connor has him working as a volunteer with me at the Bridges meetings." Renee beelined Claire's car.

"Oooo," Claire teased, following close behind. "Nothing more?"

"Not a thing."

"I should hope not," Andie said, stopping Renee steps short of the car.

Renee spun around.

"He seems nice enough," Andie said. "And no one would question his good looks, if you like that type."

Renee relaxed at Andie's qualifier. That was Andie.

Andie shook her head. "I know you both think I'm overprotective." She raised her hands Claire's way before she could comment. "I'm not just talking about his criminal record. There's something about him that says stand clear."

Renee fingered the strap of her bag while she waited for Claire to unlock the car. For once, Andie's overprotective instincts might be called for.

Chapter Six

Rhys turned the key. The truck engine hesitated before it turned over. And died. He tried again and got only a clicking sound, and then nothing. He didn't need this. Not after staying late to finish the job in Ticonderoga so the guy he was working with could leave to get to his daughter's ball game.

Rhys cranked it one more time and shoved his fingers through his hair. Even if the truck had started right away, he'd had barely enough time to get home, clean up and make the forty-five-minute drive to Elizabethtown for the Bridges' behavior management training. No way would he make it on time now. He kicked the side of the console under the dashboard. If he made it at all.

He should let someone know. Rhys pulled his phone from his pocket. *Here's another demerit*, he couldn't help but think. He'd already been a no-show at last Thursday's Bridges meeting. Owen and Dylan had still been on vacation with the Hills, and his work team had an opportunity for some overtime. He'd emailed Renee the evening before, since he didn't have her phone number. He wished email would work for today, too, so he could avoid the current of emotion he picked up when they talked. The evening at the races the week before last was a prime example.

He threw off his seat belt and yanked his phone from his pocket. Better to get this over with.

"Suzi, it's Rhys," he said when she answered.

"Hey, are you calling to talk to Owen and Dylan about the field trip to the Adirondack Museum at Blue Mountain on Saturday? They're jazzed about meeting 'real' mountain men."

Field trip? He had to work to cover his ignorance. "Meeting real mountain men? Who wouldn't be jazzed? But I can't talk with them right now. I'm in a crunch for time. Can you give me Renee's cell number?" He explained the situation.

"No problem." She rattled off the number from memory.

He scribbled it on his work pad. "Thanks. Tell Owen and Dylan I'll see them Thursday."

"I will."

Rhys ended the call and punched in Renee's number. It rang and he waited for her voice mail.

This wouldn't make him look like stellar father material. He was counting on his volunteer work with Bridges to serve as a positive when his custody hearing came up. Rhys held the phone in a viselike grip. He hated being judged on things beyond his control. The phone made an odd sound and continued to ring.

"Hello, this is Renee Delacroix."

Rhys hesitated.

"Hello?" Renee repeated.

"It's you," Rhys said. "The way you answered, I thought I'd gotten your voice mail." He rubbed the back of his neck, feeling the strain from the workday. *Smooth, Maddox. Real smooth.* "I got your number from Suzi."

"Rhys?"

"Yeah."

"I didn't recognize your number and thought it was a work call."

He grabbed the opening. "It is. I've got that training tonight, and my truck won't start. The alternator, most likely. I'm at a job site in Ticonderoga. I can probably get Pastor Connor to come pick me up and take me to get the part. But even if it's an easy fix, there's no way I can do that, get cleaned up and get to Elizabethtown for the training. Do you have the instructor's number?"

"In fact, I do." Renee rattled off a number.

"But that's…"

"My phone number. The person who was supposed to teach tonight had a family emergency, and our boss called me to fill in."

Rhys drummed his fingers on the passenger seat. He wouldn't have minded having Renee as the instructor. "All right. Then, as you heard, I'm not going to be able to make it."

"Okay, I'll cancel and reschedule the training."

Because of one person? "That seems extreme."

"You were the class. You're the only volunteer who hasn't completed the training yet." She paused. "Wait. You're in Ticonderoga?"

"On Montcalm Street."

"I could come and get you. I'm near there on my way to the office. I live in Ticonderoga. We can do the course at my place."

"I don't want to put you out." His truck would be fine here in the job parking lot until tomorrow if Pastor Connor picked him up. Then he could catch a ride into work with one of the guys and figure out what was wrong with it.

"It's not putting me out. We'll get it done, and no one will have to drive to Elizabethtown another evening. The course is online. I have access to the Action Coalition's server."

"I guess that's fine with me."

"Claire will be here, too."

Rhys smiled. That was supposed to reassure

him? "I'll check with Pastor Connor to see if he can pick me up afterward and call you back."

"I could drive you home," Renee said.

"No. Helping me get the training out of the way is enough." And wouldn't put them in the close proximity of a half-hour car ride.

"Fine. I'll be here."

Rhys called Connor and arranged for a ride home after the training. He redialed Renee, and she answered immediately.

"I'm set with Pastor Connor. He said to call when we're done."

"Good. Exactly where are you on Montcalm?"

Rhys gave her the street number. "I'm in the back parking lot."

"That's practically around the corner. I'll be there in a couple of minutes."

"Okay. I'm not going anywhere." Rhys got out of the pickup and locked the doors, for all it was worth—though probably nothing. He paced the parking lot. The heat of the day had started to fade and the cooler air on his T-shirt, still damp from work, made him all the more aware of his need to clean up. He'd have to ask Renee if he could do so at her house. All he needed was a little soap and water.

Renee pulled in next to his truck and he walked over. She hadn't been exaggerating when she'd said she was only minutes away. He opened the passenger-side door and climbed in. The light floral scent he'd begun to think of as Renee's infused the vehicle.

"I appreciate this. I need to start looking for a more reliable vehicle—a king cab for when I have the boys. But the expense has me putting it off."

"I understand."

He looked at the pristine cream-colored dashboard of her late-model sedan. He doubted it. And why had he brought up his financial situation? It was pretty obvious.

Rhys refrained from leaning back fully against the seat. "Ah, another favor? I should clean up before we do the training."

"That's no problem."

Rhys stared out the passenger-side window. Did her quick response mean he smelled? Probably. He'd been working hard all day on the building roof and dusty crawl spaces under it. He sniffed, but all he got was that floral scent. He refocused his gaze on the dashboard and rearview mirror. No air freshener—it was definitely her.

"And I'm guessing you haven't eaten," Renee said, turning onto a residential street.

"No, have you?"

She shook her head as she parked the car in front of a large Victorian home. "I was going to catch something on the way to Elizabethtown."

This is where I offer to get take-out. Rhys fingered the change in his pocket through the rough denim of his jeans. He didn't have much more in his wallet. Since Owen and Dylan had been away last week and he hadn't needed any extra money for them, he'd put nearly his whole paycheck into his truck savings fund.

"Let's see what Claire made. It was her turn to cook tonight, and she tends to cook like Mom— for nine people." Renee turned the car off and grinned. "We do a lot of leftovers when it's my night."

"Considering my cooking skills, your leftovers would trump whatever I'd be having for dinner." He opened the car door.

"No." Renee laughed. "That would be our brother Marc. He's a chef and part owner of a restaurant in New York City."

Rhys stepped out and closed the door, waiting for Renee to walk around the front of the car. "How many of you are there?"

"There's only one of me. You've met my three sisters. And Claire and I each have a twin brother. Marc is her twin and Paul is mine."

Rhys watched her approach him on the sidewalk and suppressed a smile. She was right. There was only one Renee Delacroix. And as intriguing as she could be at times, she was not his type—not by a long shot. They came from separate universes.

* * *

Renee pushed her sunglasses up on her head. It wasn't an aberration caused by the dark lenses—the usually stone-faced Rhys Maddox wore an almost goofy expression on his face. "We can be formidable en masse," she said.

"What?" He blinked.

"My family."

"Oh, yeah. I've met your parents at church."

He must be really hungry. Hungry enough to affect his attention span. She'd never seen him disoriented. They walked up the sidewalk to the house. She unlocked the door and tugged at the door handle, which was stuck.

Rhys's hand, warm and calloused, closed over hers on the handle.

"It sticks in the humidity." She slipped her hand from under his, avoiding his gaze and the uptick in her pulse rate.

He pulled the door wide open, allowing her to step inside the small entryway ahead of him and catch a cleansing breath. Wow. All he'd done was help her open the door.

"We live upstairs." She climbed the steps, unable to shake the awareness of his large form following closely behind her. If they were going to work together with the Bridges group, she had to get used to being in close proximity to him on a regular basis.

"All right, what did you forget?" Claire said in her big-sister voice as Renee opened the apartment door. Claire stopped when she noticed Rhys. "Oh, hi, Rhys."

"Claire."

Claire replaced her confused expression with a stern look at Renee. "I thought you were working tonight."

"I am. Rhys is the work," Renee said, heat warming her cheeks before she even finished getting the words out.

Claire grinned at Rhys. "And nice work when you can get it."

Rhys's lips twitched. "Renee, you said I could clean up."

Chicken. He had an escape. She pointed down a hall. "First door to the right. There are clean towels and washcloths in the cabinet."

"And so?" Claire stood in front of her, hands at her waist.

"Rhys called me to get the phone number of the person who was teaching the training tonight. He had truck trouble."

"He has your phone number?" Claire raised her eyebrows.

Renee released a sigh. "He called Suzi for my number."

"And you're here, instead of at the office, because…?"

"Rhys was working at one of the office buildings on Montcalm. That's where his truck is. I have access to the Action Coalition server on my laptop. That's where the training module is. Rhys is the only one taking it tonight. It seemed silly to drive all the way up to the office. Inquisition over?"

Claire relented. "I guess."

"Besides," Renee said, "here you can feed us. What have you got?"

"A cold tuna-macaroni salad." Claire looked thoughtful. "The ground beef I picked up on the way home is in the freezer, but not frozen yet. I can make burgers to go with the salad."

"I'm good with just the salad, but Rhys would probably like a burger," Renee said. "Hey, do you still have any of those large Experimental Farm promotional T-shirts?"

"Yeah, why?"

"One would probably fit Rhys. He could use a clean shirt. Can you get him one? I'll put on the burgers."

"Are you trying to drive him away?"

That thought had crossed her mind numerous times since she'd met the man, but not at the moment. "What do you mean?"

"I mean your attempting to cook something that can't be microwaved."

"I'm not that bad."

Claire raised her eyebrows.

"Okay," Renee said. "Where are the shirts?"

"In the box on the floor of my closet." Claire went into the kitchen, humming.

And some people envy me and my large family. Renee took a shirt from the box in Claire's room and walked up the hall to the bathroom. The sound of water running in the sink was clear through the door. She raised her hand to knock, swallowing twice to wet her dry throat before she did.

"Yes?" Rhys's voice was strained.

"I have a clean T-shirt that should fit you. The experimental farm where Claire works gave the shirts away as a promotion. She had some left over." Renee clamped her mouth shut. He didn't need the shirt's life story. "I'll leave it here in the hall."

The door opened to reveal a freshly scrubbed Rhys, his damp hair combed back from his face, the towel over his shoulder. "No, I'll take it. Thanks. I hated that I had to put this dirty one back on."

"Claire's making hamburgers and stuff," she said, her throat parched again.

"I'll change and be right there."

"The kitchen is through the living room."

"Got it." He closed the door.

She was babbling again. She rarely babbled. Renee breathed in and out. All she'd done was hand the man a shirt. And if that was enough to shred her equilibrium, how would she get through an hour or more of sitting with him at her laptop? It wasn't as if she had a projector to show the screens on the wall so she could sit across the room or walk around while she presented the information. She collected herself. *No.* She was a professional. Working with people was her job, although she mostly worked with young people.

But even at their worst, not one of the kids she'd worked with had thrown her off kilter like Rhys did.

Rhys cleaned the sink, put the body wash back where he'd found it on the side of the tub and folded the wet towel over the rack before he followed the smell of beef and fried onions to the kitchen. He really appreciated Renee and Claire's thoughtfulness and how good the clean shirt felt.

"That smells really good." His stomach growled as if to agree.

"Everything will be ready in a few minutes." Claire flipped the burgers she was cooking in an iron frying pan. While they waited, Renee placed a plate of cherry tomatoes and sliced cucumbers on the table.

"If you want to take any cucumbers or tomatoes home," Claire said, "our grandmother keeps us well supplied."

"I'll take you up on that." Rhys placed his hand

on the back of the kitchen chair closest to him. "Can I give you something for them?"

"You look like a handy guy," Claire said.

Renee's eyes narrowed.

Rhys tapped the chair back, wishing he had more skill at reading women. He had no idea how they'd gotten from his offer to pay for the tomatoes and cucumbers to Claire's remark.

"How are you at building things?"

That he knew. So he went with the flow. "It depends on what you're building."

"The landlord said we could get a dog."

"He did?" Renee interrupted. "When?"

"When I paid the rent and offered to pay extra if he let us."

"Yes," Renee said. Her gaze softened. "We always had dogs at home."

This was another Renee, different from her reserved professional and how she'd been at the motocross races. He wasn't sure how to meld them. Rhys eyed the burgers before he looked from Renee to Claire. "What does a dog have to do with building something?"

"A doghouse," they said in unison.

He should have figured that out.

"The hardware store has kits. Renee and I could manage, but it would be a snap for someone more experienced."

"Sit down. We can talk over dinner," Renee

said, opening the refrigerator. She looked over her shoulder at him. "We have iced tea and lemonade, from a can though, not fresh."

He pulled out the chair and sat. As if he'd be picky? "The lemonade is fine."

Renee poured his drink while Claire placed a plate with the burgers and a package of hamburger rolls in front of him. An off-balance warmth and feeling of uncertainty overtook him. He couldn't remember the last time he'd been fussed over like this. Maybe never. At least not since he and Gwen were newlyweds, before the boys were born and she'd had to split her attention—and her love, he'd sometimes thought selfishly. He swallowed. He had to stop thinking of Renee and Gwen at the same time. It was too dangerous a direction.

"Do you want me to say the blessing?" he asked when Renee and Claire finally settled in their seats on either side of him.

"Please," Renee said.

Before he could fold his hands, Renee and Claire reached for them. The hand-holding again. He still wasn't used to it. "Dear Lord, thank You for this bountiful food and Your hand in allowing me to share it. Amen."

"Amen." Renee and Claire immediately released his hands.

As if they'd all keep holding hands? He kept

his eyes closed an extra moment to clear his mind. He put two rolls on his plate and speared a couple of the burgers with his fork. "About the doghouse… You might do better with lumber and a plan. Kits aren't always as sturdy as you might want."

"You'd do that?" Claire asked. "We'd pay you."

Renee nodded and he shifted in his seat. "I'd be good with some more home-cooked food and…" He hesitated. "And…if you could help me get permission for Owen and Dylan to come and help me." He dropped his gaze to the sandwich he was assembling on his plate. "When Gwen—" He couldn't stop his voice from catching. "When she brought him to visit last spring, Owen went on and on about him and Josh Donnelly building his Pinewood Derby racer."

"Talk to Suzi and your caseworker. I'll let them know I'm willing to supervise. It can't hurt to ask."

First relief, and then a flood of powerlessness, washed over him. *I shouldn't have to ask.*

"Let's eat before the food gets cold." Renee scooped out a helping of macaroni salad and handed him the bowl.

Rhys concentrated on eating and let Renee and Claire talk for the rest of the meal. When he'd finished, he glanced at the clock on the coffeemaker.

"Would you like coffee?" Claire asked.

"No, thanks." *Might as well just say it.* "I'd like to get going on the training. I don't want Pastor Connor to have to come out too late to pick me up."

"Of course," Renee said.

He clenched his fists in his lap. Even if it was God's current path for him, he hated having to rely on others.

Renee hopped up to clear her plate and grabbed his, too.

"You two go ahead," Claire said. "I'll take care of the dishes."

Rhys rose. "Thanks for the food. I'll check out some doghouse plans online, price the materials and get back to you."

"Great," Claire said. "All we'll need then is the dog."

"Make yourself comfortable in the living room while I get my computer," Renee said.

He let her leave the kitchen ahead of him and went into the living room, choosing to sit in one of the side chairs that flanked the couch.

A moment later Renee and her laptop joined him. She stood at the opposite end of the coffee table, in front of the couch and chairs, and surveyed the room. "If I put the computer on the coffee table, we'll both need to sit on the couch to see the training module on the screen."

Rhys took in the two soft, overstuffed cushions

that dipped to the center of the couch, and made no motion to move.

"You know," Renee said. "It would be better if we did this at the kitchen table."

"Right." Rhys was on his feet, following Renee to the kitchen before the word was out.

"We're going to set up in here instead," Renee said when they returned to the kitchen.

"Okay. I've got the dishwasher loaded. Turn it on when you're done," Claire said. "I'll be in the living room reading the new romance novel I picked up when I was shopping."

Rhys couldn't be certain, but from the way Renee stiffened, she might have also heard Claire emphasize the word *romance*.

"All right. Let's get to work," Renee said, all business. She handed him a stapled packet of papers.

He sat and leafed through the screen shots of the training module while she booted up the laptop. No, Claire knew too much about him. She wouldn't be pushing her sister at him.

The packet looked pretty straightforward. If Renee left him to his own devices, he could be through the module and out the door in less than an hour.

She connected to the training module, tilted the computer toward him and moved her chair closer—he assumed so she could see the screen better. Why else? The evening breeze blowing through the open window above the sink wasn't doing anything to cool the room.

"You've taken online classes before?"

"Almost an entire associate's degree in general technology."

"Good. I'll read you the presenter's introduction and then leave you on your own to read the five sections and complete the questions at the end of each. If I were doing it for a group, I'd read the lead-in to each section. But you can read them as well as I can." She lifted another packet. "I've got a grant request application to work on. Isn't that crazy? They're usually all online."

He didn't know that, but almost all job applications were online, so he wasn't surprised. Rhys listened to Renee read the introduction in what he'd come to think of as her professional voice, as opposed to her tone at dinner. She finished and he waited for her to move her chair back away from the computer—and from him. She didn't. He rubbed his palm down the front of his jeans. Renee picked up a pen and went to work on her application, seemingly oblivious to him.

Rhys read the first screen through, glanced sideways at Renee, looked at the first question and went back and read it again.

Renee looked up. "Did you have a question? Feel free to ask anything. You won't interrupt me."

Did that include asking her to move around to the other side of the table? "No, I'm good."

"Then I'm going to go down to the basement to put on some laundry. Some of the information I need for this application is at work, so I can't finish it tonight."

"No problem." He focused on the intro paragraph again and held his breath until she'd left the room before diving back into the training. A short while later he heard the murmur of voices in the other room and picked up his tempo. He only needed a seventy-five to pass.

Twenty minutes later Renee still hadn't reappeared in the kitchen. The tightness in his chest loosened. Maybe she needed distance from him as much as he needed distance from her.

As if his thoughts had summoned her, Renee appeared in the doorway. "How are you doing?"

"Finishing up the last section. I was about to take a break to call Connor."

"Go ahead. I have some other things I can do. When you finish, print your certificate to HP400 and let me know. It's the wireless printer in my room."

"Got it."

Renee left, and he called Connor. To kill some time until his ride came, Rhys checked his email on his phone before answering the last two questions and submitting his training.

Ninety. Not bad. The computer asked if he wanted to go back and review and re-answer the two questions he'd missed. Rhys checked the time on the computer. Connor wouldn't be here for a few more minutes. He clicked yes.

Five minutes later the sound of the apartment door opening and a voice saying, "Hi, Pastor Connor," coincided with Rhys clicking Print for his now-perfect-score completion certificate.

He stood and walked into the living room. "All done. I printed the certificate."

"It's yours. The program will email a copy to the Bridges' director. I'll go get it." Renee was back in a flash with the printout.

"Thanks again for dinner," Rhys said. "And, Claire, I'll get those doghouse plans and estimate to you."

"Great. Rhys may build us a house for the dog we're going to get," Claire explained to Connor.

Rhys ignored the other man's raised eyebrows.

"See you Thursday," Renee said as she closed the door behind him and Connor.

"Right." He had no excuse not to be at the Bridges meeting this week. Rhys walked with Connor to the end of the sidewalk and stopped. He'd forgotten to ask Renee about the Saturday trip to the museum. Since she hadn't said anything, she must not have thought of it, either.

"Did you forget something?" Connor asked.

He could probably get the information from Pastor Connor, but didn't want to let on that he didn't know the details about the outing. Rhys waved off Connor. "Nothing I can't take care of at the meeting on Thursday." Once he'd accepted it, the Bridges gig was his responsibility. He didn't need to use Connor, or anyone else, as a crutch.

Chapter Seven

Rhys was almost as jazzed as his sons were about the mountain men reenactors and the historic logging program today at the Adirondack Museum. He looked up at the bright, almost cloudless sky above the Hazardtown Community Church parking lot. The day promised to be perfect.

Rhys had spent most of his life in the Albany area, but he'd never heard of the museum before Suzi had mentioned the trip. He'd never been to the Adirondacks until he'd been sentenced to Dannemora.

When he was growing up, trips of any kind had been rare, except for a couple of years when he'd lived with a foster family in Bethlehem. They'd taken him to museums and historic sites and to the Great Escape Amusement Park at Lake George both summers he'd been there. They'd even paid for him to swim with their son on the local private swim club. Although he'd done his best to hide it, he'd been devastated when that foster father had been transferred out of state for work. He'd kept in touch with the boy for a while, but the contact had died off.

"Daddy!" Dylan tugged on his T-shirt. "You're not listening to Miss Renee. She's talking about who's driving and who we're supposed to ride with."

"I can take four of the children in my car, and Rhys Maddox will take the rest of them and our other parent chaperone, Paige Anderson, in the church van."

"Mom," a young voice behind Rhys said, "that Rhys guy is the bad man you told me about. Dylan's father."

Rhys tensed.

"Remember, I told you he was at the Bridges meeting I went to this week. He wasn't there the first time."

It had to be the new boy who'd started coming to Bridges the week he and Dylan and Owen had missed.

A woman towing a boy about Dylan's size walked around Rhys, giving him a wide berth, and approached Renee.

"That's Tyler, the kid that told me you were a bad man," Dylan said. "He used to be my friend, but I'm not his friend anymore."

Rhys rested his hand on his younger son's shoulder. He was defending him. That had to be progress. He squeezed Dylan's shoulder, as much to dispel the combination of anger and helplessness pummeling him as to reassure his son. But he didn't want either of his boys to lose friends because of him and what he'd done.

The woman interrupted Renee and said something into her ear. Rhys could imagine what. He was well aware of what some people in the community thought of him and were saying about him and about Pastor Connor helping him relocate in Paradox Lake. But those people seemed to be a minority.

Renee frowned and nodded. "Okay, Tyler, Emma, Melody and Serge will ride with me. Everyone else is in the van with Mr. Rhys and Mrs. Anderson."

"That means we're riding with Dad," Owen said.

"I know that," Dylan said. "I'm glad Emma is riding with Miss Renee. She talks to me too much."

Me, too, and her mother, as well, Rhys thought. He and Kari had been the first ones to arrive at the church this morning. The way Kari had pulled in right behind him almost made him wonder if she had been waiting in her driveway until he'd gone by her house, except he had no idea if he'd driven by her house.

"Dylan, that wasn't very nice. Emma is just friendly."

Dylan pulled away and Rhys clenched his teeth. Because he'd reprimanded Dylan, was he going to ask to ride with Renee now, even though Emma would be in the car, too? How would that go over with Tyler's mother?

"Come on, Dylan," Owen said. "I'll race you to the van."

He probably should have discouraged them from running, but Owen's challenge had snapped Dylan out of it. "Line up by the van with Mrs. Anderson," Renee called to the boys jostling for position beside the side door of the vehicle. Mr. Rhys will be right there."

Her nearness startled him. He'd been focused on his sons and hadn't noticed her approach.

"Don't let her get to you." Rhys didn't have to ask who. "She has a knack for sucking the sunshine out of any gathering." She tapped his arm. "Let's see if we can put it back in."

This was the Cheerleader Renee he'd met at the motocross races that he had trouble reconciling with the Oh-So-Professional Renee he'd first met at CPS.

"She didn't bother me," he said. *Much.* "I'm sure I've heard whatever she said before."

Renee pursed her lips, giving Rhys a picture of what she might have looked like when she was Emma's age and someone had done something she'd objected to. But cute as that picture—past and present—was, he didn't need Renee to fight his battles for him.

"We'd better get to the cars before we have a riot," she said. "We have some very excited little boys and girls on our hands."

Rhys looked over at the boys hopping and Emma twirling around beside the vehicles. Even shy little Melody had a big grin on her face rather than her usual withdrawn expression.

"And." Renee fingered her silver cross. "We have a couple of guys who look like they'd rather be anywhere but here."

He caught sight of Serge and another older boy off to the side looking disdainful. "No," Rhys disagreed. "I know that look." He should. He'd spent years perfecting it to protect himself from disappointment. "My guess is that they're almost as excited as the younger kids, but too cool to show it."

"That's what I was hoping. I'd like you to take them in your group when we split up at the museum for the tour and hands-on activities."

"Sure, along with Owen and Dylan."

Renee's lips parted as if she was going to say something.

"Is that a problem?"

"No. I was just thinking Dylan might want to be with the younger kids." Her voice rose at the end of the sentence, indicating a question or nerves. "Some of the activities are age-based."

He shrugged. "We'll see what he wants to do."

Renee looped her arm through his to walk across the parking lot. He didn't know whether it was her exuberance for the outing or a reward for his saying the right thing. But it didn't matter. It made him feel like he and his sons belonged, at least for the time being.

"There it is! I can see the sign!" Emma shouted in a voice loud enough for the people in the car ahead of them to hear.

"Yes, it is." Renee couldn't believe how quickly the fifty-minute drive to Blue Mountain Lake and the museum had gone by. And despite the car vibrating with their excitement, the kids had been well behaved, better than she and her siblings had been on some trips her family had taken.

Emma twisted around. "And Mr. Rhys is still behind us."

"I expected he would be." Renee pulled into a parking space in the museum parking lot. "Everyone stay buckled in and in the car until Mr. Rhys has the van parked and I say so."

Rhys pulled in next to her.

"Okay." She gave the go-ahead. "Stay beside the car. We're going to walk into the museum together."

The kids tumbled out of the car to mingle with the others who'd ridden with Rhys. As was Building Bridges' policy, Renee took a head count and checked off each child on a clipboard. "Let's head in. Line up single-file."

The younger kids scrambled to be first, while the two fifth-grade boys took their time sauntering from the van over to the end of the line.

"Mr. Rhys, would you follow up in the back?"

"Sure thing." He smiled before stepping over next to the two boys, one of his rare real smiles that made Renee think there was a lot more to Rhys than he let on. It made her want to know him better.

"Follow me," Renee said, leading them into the museum entrance.

The woman at the admission desk greeted them. "You must be the Building Bridges group."

"How did you know that?" Emma asked.

The woman eyed their matching lime-green T-shirts. "Your shirts, honey."

"Oh, yeah."

"I have you down for three adults and nine children. Is that right?"

"All present and accounted for." Renee handed her the Building Bridges' debit card to pay for their admissions.

"Your tour guide will be here in a minute." The woman handed the card back to Renee a minute later and looked over the group again. "After the orientation tour, I suggest you break into older and younger groups. Some of the hands-on mountain man activities have a minimum age."

"Okay, thanks."

When she turned back to the group, Rhys walked up to her and motioned for Paige to join them. Was something wrong?

"I know we didn't talk about it beforehand, but I think it would be a good idea if we go with a buddy system as well as breaking into age groups," he said.

"It would." She should have thought of that. She was the person in charge. Renee took in Rhys's clear, steady gaze. *No, we're a team.* The Hazardtown Building Bridges team. She cleared her throat. "Everyone listen up. I want each of you to choose a buddy for the day."

Emma jumped up and down, her hand in the air. "Like we do at school when we go to lunch, hold hands and walk together? I want to be Mr. Rhys's buddy, unless he's going to be your buddy, Miss Renee."

The air in the museum seemed to crackle as Renee remembered the feel of Rhys's strong, calloused hand gripping hers when he'd said grace before dinner the other night.

"Mr. Rhys and I will look out for each other." Her cheeks warmed as she hastily added, "And Mrs. Anderson. I meant for you to choose another child as your buddy."

"But there are nine kids," Emma said. "You can't divide nine by two."

The older boys snickered. A look from Rhys was enough to quell them. Emma was too cute and too smart for her own good.

"I have a solution," Renee said. "We'll divide into our two groups first. Everyone who's going into fourth or fifth grade is in Mr. Rhys's group."

Four boys, including Owen and Serge, shuffled toward Rhys.

"Emma, Melody, Tyler, Noah and Dylan are with Mrs. Anderson and me." Renee shot Rhys an apologetic look. He shrugged. "Now, everyone choose buddies. I'd rather not assign them."

"I choose Noah because I don't want to be with a girl," Tyler said, his belligerent tone making Melody cringe.

"I'll be Melody's buddy 'cause she's little and I can look after her," Dylan said quietly, ignoring the other boy's dig.

"That's very nice of you," Renee said.

Tyler pulled a face at Dylan. Renee prayed the whole afternoon wouldn't go like this.

"And Emma's buddy, too," he said. "If I have to."

Seeing the same protective trait in Dylan that she'd seen in Rhys for his sons tugged at her heart.

"That's okay with me," Emma said. "We can both be Melody's buddy and take care of her. We're six."

"Thank you, Emma. Is everyone paired up?" Rhys's gaze held hers until the connection became a line pulling her into murky waters. And the waters didn't get any murkier than Rhys.

"Hi, I'm Talia, your guide." A bubbly young woman introduced herself to the group.

"Renee Delacroix, from Building Bridges, and my volunteers Paige Anderson and Rhys Maddox." She ignored the irritation that poked her when Talia cast Rhys a wide smile.

The tour lasted about forty minutes, almost too long for some of the younger kids. But lunch at the museum's Lakeview Café with ice cream for dessert revived them. They broke into their two groups afterward to try the special children's activities staffed by volunteer mountain men and loggers.

Toward the end of the afternoon, everyone met up at the last two activities. The younger children were trying their hand at poling logs down a model of the Schroon River, and the older boys testing their strength wielding rubber mallets on a machine that measured how many ax strikes they'd need to chop the branches off a felled tree to ready it to float downstream.

"Hey, Dad," Owen said when he'd finished his turn. "Why don't you take a try?"

"No, it's for you guys." Rhys motioned at Owen and the other boys in his group.

"Come on, Mr. Rhys. Show us your stuff," Serge joined in.

"Go ahead. Give it a try," the reenactor staffing the activity, said. "There's no one else waiting."

"Isn't it a kid thing?" Rhys asked, checking out the guy's nametag—Jeff.

"No," Jeff said. "Tell you what. Why don't we have a friendly competition? I could use the exercise. I'll go first. You see if you can beat me."

Rhys hesitated.

"Do it, Dad."

"Yeah, Mr. Rhys," the other three boys said in chorus.

"Okay." Rhys relented.

"Dylan, Miss Renee!" Owen shouted. "You've gotta see this. Dad is going to try to beat the logger guy."

Renee looked over from where she was helping Melody finish guiding her log down the river and waved. "Be there in a minute." This was something she wouldn't mind watching.

"I'll take the kids over and Emma to the

ladies' room while you and Melody finish here," Paige said.

"I'll be real fast," Emma said, hopping around more than usual. "I don't want to miss Mr. Rhys."

"Thanks, Paige."

Melody skipped beside Renee as they moved to join the others.

"Honey, your shoe's coming untied." Renee stopped her.

"Can you tie it? It takes me too long. I want to see Mr. Rhys."

Didn't they all? Renee knelt and glanced over at the boys standing wide-eyed while the burly reenactor began making quick work of trimming the virtual tree.

"All done," Renee said. She stood and took Melody's hand. With a satisfied smile, the reenactor handed Rhys the mallet.

"Wait, Dad," Owen said as Rhys accepted the mallet. "Wait for Miss Renee."

"And Mrs. Anderson and Emma," Renee called back. Emma would never forgive any of them if she missed watching Mr. Rhys.

"Your father should be real good at this," Tyler said.

Renee's ears perked up. Was Tyler saying something nice to Dylan? The boy had tried to belittle Dylan during every activity and to get his buddy to do the same. She was going to talk with the director and Pastor Connor about Tyler. She certainly didn't want to deprive Tyler of the benefits of the group, but constant disruption and bullying wasn't good for the other children.

"Him being in prison, he probably got a lot of practice smashing rocks with a sledgehammer like on cartoons."

"Did not," Dylan said. "Mommy took us to visit him there. They don't smash rocks."

"Ha, ha, I'm going to tell everyone in first grade that you've been to prison, learning to be a criminal just like your father. No one will be your friend, right, Noah?"

At Noah's agreement, Dylan's face crumpled. Renee broke into a jog that Melody could keep up with. Why wasn't Rhys doing something? She looked at him. He stood as still as a granite mountain, the devastated look on his face rivaling the one on his younger son's face. Her heart tore in two.

"Leave Dylan alone." Owen lunged at Tyler. Renee dropped Melody's hand and broke into a run.

Rhys caught Owen by the neck of his T-shirt with one hand and held his other arm out, fingers splayed to block Tyler's rush toward Owen. "Stop. Violence doesn't solve anything." His voice was low and held no anger, only solid steel.

It wasn't exactly how she would have handled

things, or even close. Her training had emphasized encouraging touch. But Rhys had been effective. Both boys stood still, glaring at each other. Renee caught her breath and placed her hand on Tyler's shoulder, tightening her grip when he tried to shake it off. She'd admit that Rhys might know more about getting through to boys than she did.

"I didn't miss it, did I?" Emma trotted up with Mrs. Anderson behind her.

Rhys released a mirthless laugh, along with the hold on Owen's shirt.

"Mr. Rhys with the hammer," Emma clarified.

"No, sweetie, you didn't miss anything with the hammer," Renee answered. *At least not the hammer you mean.* "Tyler, please walk to the van with me."

The boy shot Rhys and Owen a nasty scowl.

"Now," she said.

Tyler started toward the parking lot with her. In the background, Renee heard the repeated ding of the bell signaling Rhys's hammer blows. She wouldn't be surprised if the brute strength earned him a museum record.

What did surprise her, however, was the deep reassurance his show of strength gave her.

I will not be the example for Owen and Dylan that kid said I am. Rhys silently repeated the phrase with each slam of the mallet until a blast of bells and whistles signaled that he'd trimmed his tree.

"Nice job. You win," Jeff said as Rhys handed him the mallet. "In fact, that might be a museum record."

Rhys nodded.

"Everyone line up with his or her buddy," Mrs. Anderson said. "It's time to go. Thank Jeff for the good time."

Rhys wiped the sweat from his brow. *Mostly good time.* He probably should have said what Paige had. It was his group's activity.

"Wait, Dad," Owen said as Rhys started toward the end of the line to follow the kids to the vehicles.

"What?"

"You should get a badge like we did."

"So you should," Jeff said with a grin. He handed Rhys the stick-on circular badge the boys in Rhys's group each sported.

"Put it on," Owen and Serge said.

Rhys peeled off the paper back and slapped the badge on his T-shirt.

Paige smiled her admiration.

But instead of her pleasant, attractive face, Rhys couldn't help visualizing Renee's beautiful one, all smiles when he'd completed the behavior modification training at her house the other eve-

ning with a perfect score. He pulled at the neck-
line of his sticky shirt. Despite the time with his
sons, today's trip couldn't be over soon enough.

"Dylan's riding back with me," Rhys announced when they met Renee and a very sul-
len-looking Tyler in the parking lot.

"Okay," Dylan said quietly.

Rhys shoved his hands into his front pockets.
He was the father. Right now, he didn't care if
his son wanted to ride with Renee or if Renee
thought he should ride with her. He didn't want
him with Tyler.

"Of course," Renee said. "He rode here with
you."

The remaining tension Rhys hadn't pounded
out of himself with the mallet drained from him.
He didn't know what he expected her to say. But
whether it was her intention or not, Renee's words
validated Rhys's actions as a father, even if those
actions may not have been recommended in the
Building Bridges' handbook.

Renee pulled out her clipboard and checked off
the kids as they took their seats in each vehicle.

The kids were quieter on the way home, their
excitement and energy spent, which made the
trip seem much longer without their enthusiastic chatter.

When he pulled into the church parking lot,
Rhys was glad to see all of the parents there

waiting to pick up their children. He wondered if Renee was glad, too. Today had been an experience for him, in more ways than one.

Out of the corner of his eye, he saw Renee escort Tyler to his mother as he walked Owen and Dylan to Jack Hill, who was waiting beside his truck.

The usual sense of loss spread through Rhys's gut.

"Rhys."

"Jack."

"Did you guys have a good time?" Jack asked.

"The best," Owen said. "You should have seen Daddy hammer through the tree trimming activity. He beat the logger guy, probably set a record. He's really strong."

Jack nodded, a smile twitching the corners of his lips.

Rhys shifted his weight.

"Yeah," Dylan said softly. "And he made Tyler stop saying mean things to me."

Nothing he'd had to contend with while in prison—or anywhere else—had ever made him as weak-kneed as Dylan's quiet statement.

"Without hitting Tyler or anything," Dylan added, "like Owen was going to."

Molten iron ran through him. How would Jack take Dylan's implication that he might consider that? He'd never hit his sons or any other child since he'd been a child himself.

"Daddy said vi-lence doesn't solve anything." Dylan brought Rhys down off the ledge. Since when had he cared what other people thought of him?

"Like we learned in vacation Bible school," Owen said. "Turn the other cheek. But I think Daddy's loud voice scared Tyler out of saying anything else."

"Sounds like you had quite a day," Jack said, opening the back door to his pickup. "All of you."

Jack's gaze held his while the boys climbed in the truck, and Rhys experienced an alien feeling, one he'd had very few times before—male camaraderie that didn't have any expectations.

"'Bye, Daddy." His boys waved out the open window as Jack climbed in the truck.

"'Bye, guys. See you at church tomorrow."

He watched them drive off, followed by the last of the other parents.

"Rhys," Renee said.

He started. "Dylan told Jack that I made Tyler stop being mean to him." He scuffed his toe on the asphalt. He had no idea why he'd blurted that out, except for the difficulty he was having processing the feelings Dylan's words had released in him. "The Building Bridges stuff may be working," he said to cover himself.

"I'd say that's progress. Congrats." Renee's gaze flickered around the parking lot, as if making sure no one was listening to them. "I know you're probably anxious to get home but…"

Was she going to ask him to do something with her this evening? Dinner at her place with Claire again? He forced out a hitched breath. The stress of the day must have made him delusional.

"I talked with Tyler's mother about his behavior and have a strong feeling she's going to call the Bridges' director to complain about how Tyler was treated."

"She's going to call and complain about us?" His disbelief made him pause between each word. "Seriously?"

"I'm afraid so. We have to fill out a form about the incident, anyway, so unless you have other plans for the evening, I'd like to take the time now and have it on the director's desk before Tyler's mother calls him."

"Here?"

"No." She looked at him strangely.

Of course not. If he'd been talking with her on the phone instead of in person, he'd have slapped himself on the side of the head. The day had taken more out of him than he'd thought. If this was day-to-day parenting, he had his work cut out for him—not that the thought in any way diminished his determination to regain full custody of Owen and Dylan.

"Do you have a laptop?" she asked.

"Yeah." He'd picked up a refurbished one last paycheck in anticipation of having custody of Owen and Dylan in a few months, figuring Owen at least would need one for school. He planned to have cable internet service installed next payday.

"The form is online. You could stop by your house, pick up your laptop and meet me at the Paradox Lake General Store. They have Wi-Fi. We can grab a table and fill it out there. Get something to eat."

"All right. See you there." He wasn't even going to think about suggesting they do the form at his house, not with the way his insides churned around her at the least expected times. Besides, he had nothing to offer her to eat.

Rhys waited until she pulled out of her parking space and followed her out. She turned toward the highway and he headed down Hazard Cove Road. He would have liked to show her the house he'd rented for Owen and Dylan and himself. Memories of his pregnant wife and him walking through the house they'd bought in Albany before Dylan was born, and talking about how perfect it was for their family, flooded his mind. Rhys winced. Renee wasn't Gwen. He had no reason to show her what a great place his rental was for Owen and Dylan.

Rhys hit the steering wheel. Renee not only got his insides churning, she also messed with his head, making her one dangerous woman.

Chapter Eight

A week later Rhys leaned against the side of his truck in the Tops parking lot waiting for Renee. He touched the back pocket of his jeans and fingered the edge of the letter from Family Court folded inside. The letter had thrown him like a sucker punch to his solar plexus. His initial plan after reading it had been to crack open his Bible for some guidance on anger control—done—and to give himself some time to cool down—hence the grocery trip—and then to show the letter to the Hills this afternoon for his scheduled visit with Owen and Dylan. That was before he'd seen Renee's car in the parking lot whcn hc'd come out with his groceries.

Within a couple of minutes, Renee exited the store and stopped out front beside the row of returned carts. She eyed her bags. Rhys pushed away from his truck and closed the distance between them in several long strides.

"Need some help?" he asked as he came up behind her and reached for the bag she'd lifted out of the cart.

"Eek!" The bag slipped from her hand before she could add it to the one she gripped in her other hand. It hit the asphalt, sending a head of cabbage and several nectarines careening toward the cars.

Rhys dashed out into the parking lot and retrieved the last of the nectarines just before it rolled under a van. "I didn't mean to scare you." He held out the produce, feeling himself shrink before her eyes when he took in the dirt and gravel on the cabbage leaves, and the split and bruised fruit. "I'll replace them."

"No, it's fine." She opened the bag and waited for him to drop the vegetables in.

He pulled out his wallet, a conciliatory, "I insist," on the tip of his tongue.

Before he could get the words out, her eyes grew wide. Her gaze had darted from his face to the parking lot beside him. His letter lay on the asphalt, the Family Court insignia clearly visible. He scooped it up and ordered his thoughts.

Rhys Maddox didn't grovel. Ask anyone who knew him at Dannemora or anywhere else. But this was his kids. And he needed someone with authority on his side. He didn't know who to turn to except Renee. She knew him and his sons as well as anyone here—anyone anywhere—and had experience with the workings of CPS. Rhys stared at the court insignia and his heart slammed against his chest. He was about to grovel as he'd never groveled before.

"Want to go someplace to talk?" Renee nodded at a woman with two kids walking past them.

He breathed in and completely filled his lungs for the first time since he'd opened his mailbox this morning. "Yes. Where?" He'd suggest the coffee shop, but he didn't think his nerves needed any more caffeine.

"At the park. The bench by the waterfall. Give me a few minutes to pick up a prescription for my grandmother at the drugstore. I'll meet you after that."

He nodded, lifting the remaining bags of groceries from her cart and carrying them to her car in silence.

"Thanks," she said, popping open the trunk. "See you in a few minutes."

Since he had time to kill, Rhys left his truck in the parking lot in favor of walking the few blocks to the park to grind the edge off his anger, fear and helplessness. He repeated to himself Isaiah 41:13, one of the passages he'd read this morning.

"For I the Lord thy God will hold your right hand, saying unto thee, 'Fear not, I will help thee.'"

The Lord knew he needed all the help he could get, understood how much of a work in progress he was. He swallowed his pride and distrust of authority. If he was going to get Renee and Social Services behind him, he might have to crack open the man behind the iron bars, a person he'd revealed to God but had allowed no one else to see except Gwen and his boys.

Renee passed him and pulled her car onto a side street next to the park. He crossed US Route 9 and joined her at the waterfall. She motioned to the bench where she sat, on the side closest to the water.

He pulled the court letter from his pocket and sat. *Calm, rational, open*, Rhys counseled himself before speaking. "I've done everything everyone has asked me to do concerning Owen and Dylan, and this is what I get." He lifted the letter to wave it at her, then thought better and dropped his hand to the bench.

"I—" Renee started.

"Let me finish. Please." *Before I chicken out.* "I'm a man who takes care of his own. I don't ask for help."

Renee's expression remained placid.

She could be placating him, but he took it as a good sign and felt his tension level go down a couple of degrees. He *was* stating the obvious. "I've rented us a good place, a house with three bedrooms. It's in the Schroon Lake school district, so Owen and Dylan won't have to change schools. I have a job, a good job, and I've talked to Neal about staying local. I haven't missed a single scheduled visit with my guys. I have spots reserved at the Hazardtown Community Church day care. I followed Pastor Connor's suggestion that I volunteer with Building Bridges. I've been taking it slow and easy with Dylan like you and Suzi told me to." He reached for anything he was missing, hating the note of desperation that had crept into his voice.

"Now this." Rhys unfolded the letter and pushed it toward Renee. "I need your help making sense of it." He pressed his back against the hard wooden slats.

Renee scanned the paper. "It's a notice to appear in Family Court a week from Monday."

"I know." He might not have the education she had, but he could read. "What I don't know is why. After I petitioned for Owen and Dylan's custody, at the fact-finding hearing, Social Services recommended a postponement of the dispositional hearing for three months to allow the boys and me to get reacquainted. My lawyer convinced me to agree. The disposition is still nearly ten weeks away." *Nine weeks and two days, to be exact.*

Rhys moved to the edge of the bench and motioned toward the letter. "It has to be something CPS did, something they told the court. I know it's not coming from Jack and Suzi." A thought made his stomach sink. *Tyler's mother.* Did the Building Bridges' director contact CPS? "What's going on? You've got to help me here."

She shook her head. "No."

The bench shook with the sudden change as Rhys propelled himself to his feet.

He stood, towering over her. "What?"

Her first thought, despite his show, was that Rhys wasn't the dangerous man she'd initially thought he was. She knew now where that dangerous aura came from—an overpowering desire to have his sons back, not from whom he'd been in the past.

"I meant, no, the director was fine with our report. He wouldn't have contacted CPS. We didn't do anything that intentionally violated the Building Bridges' procedures, and I told him about other behavior problems I've observed with Tyler. I can't see anything you've done that would trigger a hearing. If you had, I think your CPS caseworker would have contacted you. You have been checking your email?"

"Yes, every day."

She saw both Owen and Dylan in his sheepish expression.

Rhys dropped back onto the bench and held his head in his hands. "Read it again. Please." He lifted his head.

His eyes, which she'd previously found so cold, stared into hers as if he could ferret out the answer he wanted there. They were bleak, not cold. She reread the letter.

"Well?" He leaned toward her and she resisted pulling back. No matter what his background, here, now, Rhys was a man—a parent—in pain.

"It's a standard notice."

His shoulders slumped. "You don't know what this court date is about." It was a statement not a question.

"No." She dropped her hand from her lap to the bench between them. "You have a lawyer, right? Did you contact him or her?" She was sure he would have, but needed to say something.

"Yes, the court appointed one for me. It's the weekend. I called and left a message." He tapped his foot on the ground in front of the bench.

"The letter isn't necessarily bad," she said.

He straightened. "I know."

Renee hesitated, gathering her thoughts before she said the first thing that popped into her mind. She didn't work at CPS anymore. There might be something about Rhys that had come to light since she'd left.

"You don't know how hard I've prayed it's not about denying my petition for custody."

Renee knew about Rhys's rebirth and baptism in prison and hated the seed of skepticism she harbored about his prison conversion. She acknowledged her shortcoming. *Lord, help me. I know I should be more forgiving and accepting.*

"I'll put you and the boys in my prayers. My Meme..."

His brow wrinkled at the unfamiliar French-Canadian word.

"My grandmother is on the prayer chain at Hazardtown Community. I can ask her to put you on it."

"No!" His voice boomed over the muted sounds of the other people in the park. He softened it. "No thanks. It's private. I'm private. I'm well aware that there are people at church, others in town like Tyler's mother, who don't believe I've changed. People who think I'm faking my faith to get custody, that I used it to get my job, whatever. I'll deal with it."

She winced when she realized she might fall into that group. "That doesn't stop me from praying for you."

His jaw relaxed and his eyes softened. "No, it doesn't."

Warmth flowed through her, and she looked up at the midday sun, acknowledging that not all of the heat was solar.

"I'm going to show Jack and Suzi the letter when I go over for dinner tonight, see if they know anything."

"Good plan." She stood to leave. "Do you want a lift back to your truck?"

"No." He smiled what she'd come to think of as his true smile, the one he gave Owen and Dylan. "I'll walk. I'm just killing time until my visit at the Hills' later. See you at church tomorrow."

She didn't want to decipher why his *no* struck her as a rebuff or why she should care. Her only connection to him was as her Bridges volunteer. "Right. Your caseworker and lawyer should have information for you on Monday."

His shoulders slumped. "I'm sure they will."

Renee watched Rhys head out of the park. She honked and waved as she drove past him on her way to Meme's, self-doubt creeping into her. The director hadn't questioned anything in their report. She'd thought it had showed Rhys in a good light, and she'd touched on behavior problems she'd had with Tyler at the two meetings he'd attended so far. She blew a puff of air that ruffled her bangs.

Ten minutes later she pulled into the driveway

of her grandmother's house on a small side road near Paradox Lake.

Meme met her at the door. "Thanks for picking up my medicine, honey." She held the screen door for Renee. "Come in. I have our lunch all ready."

"You didn't have to do that. I had to come to Paradox Lake today anyway to drop off the vacuum bag I picked up for Natalie in Ticonderoga. It only took me an extra few minutes to swing from the parsonage to the pharmacy for you. And I got some specials at Tops while I was there."

"Ah." Meme ushered her into the kitchen. "But this way I get to catch up with you. I don't see as much of you or Claire since you moved to Ticonderoga."

Renee slid into one of two seats set for lunch. "You can have me all afternoon. I have nothing planned except helping Claire clean the apartment."

Her grandmother opened the oven door and Renee's stomach rumbled at the mouthwatering scent of her grandmother's homemade macaroni and cheese. "Excuse me."

Meme waved her off. "You're hungry." She eyed Renee. "You girls don't eat enough." Meme placed one casserole dish on the table and lifted a second one out. "I made one for you to take home."

"You're the best." Renee poured herself and her

grandmother each a glass of lemonade from the pitcher on the table. Real lemonade, from fresh lemons. Her mind went back to dinner with Rhys and Claire when she'd apologized to him for having lemonade from a can.

Before taking the seat across from her, Meme scooped a large helping of macaroni and cheese onto Renee's plate and a smaller helping onto her own. She sat and offered thanks before lifting her fork. "So, who did you see at the store this morning? You and Claire aren't the only ones I haven't seen much of this week, being laid up with that summer bug I've had."

Renee gave herself a moment to enjoy the comforting taste of cheese, cream and butter on her tongue before answering. "Mainly tourists and Rhys Maddox."

"I was glad to see him at church last week," her grandmother said. "He'd been coming regularly with Suzi and Jack Hill and his little boys, and then he stopped going for a while."

The hint of censure in Meme's voice made Renee come to Rhys's defense. "He was working in Watertown for a couple of weeks." But that was several weeks ago, and she could remember him missing only one Sunday during that time, not that she was counting.

"Hmm." Meme nibbled on a half forkful of macaroni.

To escape her grandmother's probing gaze, Renee pushed her food around her plate. When she looked up, Meme was still studying her. "What do you think of Rhys?" Renee asked, the words bursting from her of their own accord. She scooped up a mouthful of food as much to keep herself from randomly blurting out anything else as to fill her empty insides.

Meme laughed. "I think he's one fine-looking man. If I were fifty years younger…"

Renee choked down her food. "Meme!"

"What? His dark, brooding looks remind me of your Pepe when he was young."

Renee couldn't argue. Rhys *was* attractive, if you liked dark, brooding and taciturn. She raised her napkin to hide the warm, indulgent smile her grandmother's indignation and dreamy expression had brought to her lips. *No need to encourage this line of conversation.* She knew Meme's thoughts on her and Claire finding "a nice young man."

"I meant his coming to church, whether it's sincere or a show to get custody of his kids," Renee said. "Some people at Hazardtown Community have questioned his membership."

Meme placed her fork on the table, fingers splayed over it, and pinned her gaze on Renee. "I think a man's relationship with God is between him and God."

Meme's reprimand made her feel ten years old, as it should. "Of course, you're right." Rhys's beliefs, custody petition, his relationship with Owen and Dylan and theirs with him—none of it, beyond their participation in the Bridges program, was her business. She sipped her lemonade, the tang of the fruit overpowering the sweetness of the sugar Meme had added.

She wouldn't allow herself to read more into her relationship with Rhys—as she'd done with the medic in Haiti—than there was to it. The sooner she let go and instructed her feelings to stay where they belonged, the better off they'd all be.

Monday morning Rhys sat in the County Social Services' office, tapping his foot in anticipation of meeting with his caseworker, Ms. Bulmer. He'd talked with Suzi and Jack. They'd had no more idea what might have precipitated the Family Court notice than he had. All they'd known was that Ms. Bulmer had had a death in the family and hadn't been in the office last week.

"Mr. Maddox." Ms. Bulmer appeared in the waiting room doorway, looking more frazzled than he'd seen her the few other times they'd talked in person. He didn't know if that—or the fact that he hadn't had to wait long to see her—was a good sign or a bad one.

"I'm sorry," she said as she led him to one of the cubicles at the far side of the room. She sat and opened the folder she'd held. "My father died last Monday. I was out of the office all week."

Rhys held tight to his impatience. "I'm sorry for your loss."

"Thank you. You should have received a letter from me early last week. I drafted it Monday and left a message when I called in Tuesday to send it to you. The letter never went out." She lifted her hands, palms up, in entreaty. "We're more short-staffed than usual. We haven't been able to replace Ms. Delacroix."

"I understand. Ms. Delacroix would be hard to replace."

His caseworker gave him a funny look.

What had he said wrong? He had no doubt Renee would have had that letter out to him on Tuesday. Best he keep quiet and only answer questions.

"We need to place another child with Jack and Suzi Hill. This child has special emotional needs that necessitate our removing your sons from their home, for their welfare as well as the other child's."

Rhys leaned forward. Another foster home? How did that require a Family Court hearing? He bit back his questions and the other thoughts racing through his mind.

"I know the Hills have been a good fit for..." Ms. Bulmer glanced at the open folder. "Owen and Dylan."

He gripped the edge of the table. She had to check their names?

"But the Hills are the only foster parents we have with the necessary training to care for the other child. You understand?"

Not at all. He nodded.

"So, we've recommended a provisional placement with..."

Rhys gripped the table tighter.

"You."

His tension snapped like a cut support cable, leaving him dangling in the wind. "With me." He had to make sure he'd heard right.

The caseworker smiled. "With you. That's what the hearing notice you received is about."

His heart filling to bursting, Rhys closed his eyes for a quick, *Thank You, Lord*, before he thanked the caseworker.

She smiled again. "I'd like to take the credit. My days tend to have too little good news to share. But you've had good reports from the Hills, a solid recommendation from Pastor Connor Donnelly and your older boy has expressed a preference to live with you."

Rhys couldn't keep the silly grin from his face, even as he asked, "And Dylan?"

"Your younger son is still conflicted. Mr. Richards, the children's law guardian, didn't press him for his preference, especially since the Hills wouldn't be part of that choice. We believe it's best that the boys stay together."

"That's a given. I mean, I agree, and we're doing the Building Bridges thing."

"Yes, we've recommended your continued participation be one of the custody provisions. You'll have those resources."

Including Renee. The reality that he was going to get Owen and Dylan took a firmer hold on him. And the thought of Renee helping, working with him and the boys, brought a wash of calm that helped him control the joy inside him. He really shouldn't leap from his chair, fist-pumping and shouting *Yes!* He could do that later.

"You'll also have the Hills. They've said they'd be happy to stay in contact with you and your sons."

Rhys thought of the connection he'd made with Jack after the Bridges' field trip. "And Jack Hill's mother—we all go to the same church and she works at the child-care center—has become a surrogate grandmother to Owen and Dylan. They don't really have any grandparents."

"That's good." Ms. Bulmer straightened the papers in Rhys's folder and closed it.

Rhys took that as a sign they were done,

pushed his chair from the table and stood. The grandmother bit was probably overkill, but it had just come out of his mouth like so many other things lately.

Ms. Bulmer rose and offered her hand. "Good luck."

"Thanks again." He turned away and then back. "Wait. Can I tell Owen and Dylan?"

"No, their law guardian is meeting with them and the Hills later today."

"Oh, okay." The reminder that others still had control tarnished his unbridled happiness. But he knew he had to play by the rules.

When he was safely in his truck, he let go with the "whoop" he'd been restraining. Rhys pulled his cell phone from his pocket, ready to call Renee with the news.

He stopped. That might be assuming too much of their friendship.

He'd need to talk with her about being a character witness, anyway. Or his lawyer would, if he needed character witnesses.

No, he'd call Pastor Connor. He was the person who'd gotten him here. Yeah, he'd call Connor. Then, he needed to get to work. He'd already lost a couple of hours. Now, more than ever, he needed to focus on his sons and their welfare—not on being friends with Renee.

Chapter Nine

Rhys tugged at his necktie to no avail. It still felt like a noose around his neck. *Might as well get it over with.* He stepped out of his truck onto the sidewalk in front of the courthouse, the already-sweltering morning sun baking him in his dark wool suit, the only one he had.

"Rhys."

He looked over his shoulder to see Connor Donnelly striding up the sidewalk toward him. "Pastor Connor." Rhys extended his hand. "I really appreciate this."

"No problem. It's part of the job."

Despite Connor's smile, Rhys felt a letdown. What had he expected? That the pastor was here strictly for him, that he had no agenda? Pastor Connor was a great guy. But Rhys was well aware that Connor considered him one of, if not the, star "save" from the Christian Action Coalition's prison ministry that Connor led.

"I talked with your lawyer yesterday. She knows I'm available as a character witness."

Rhys swallowed his doubt. "I don't know what to say." All he'd asked Connor for was moral support. On his lawyer's advice, he'd backed down from his earlier idea of asking Pastor Connor, the Hills and Renee to testify on his behalf. Ms. Johnson had said it might be overkill and prolong the hearing. Rhys was all for getting it over with, but not to the point of short-changing him and his boys. A vision of another court-appointed attorney making short work of his defense obscured his hope. Then, his sons had had their mother. This time, more was at stake. He blew out a breath. But the attorney knew the judge, and these kinds of proceedings, better than he did.

"You don't need to say anything." Pastor Connor slapped his back. "Let's go in and wrap this up."

Ms. Johnson was seated at the front of the courtroom, along with Mr. Richards, the law guardian appointed to represent Owen and Dylan's interests, the Hills and—Rhys almost missed a step. Renee. The professional Renee in her sharply creased dress slacks, blouse and short-sleeved jacket.

Since he'd met with his caseworker, he'd

avoided personal contact with her so he could keep his mind clear. He'd helped with the Bridges meeting on Thursday, but had left right after. When Claire had checked in with him about the doghouse, he'd put her off, saying he was getting in as much overtime at work as he could before Owen and Dylan came to live with him. It was true. He had been.

A chill ran through Rhys. Could Renee be here representing the Action Coalition and Building Bridges? Something related to Tyler and his mother? Ms. Johnson had contacted the director of the Building Bridges' program for a report on his and Dylan's progress and Rhys's volunteering. But Renee had said the other day that the director had accepted their report with no questions. He clenched his jaw, trying to drive out the feeling that he and Renee were back to Ms. Delacroix and Mr. Maddox.

Rhys held his index finger up when Ms. Johnson motioned him to her, and walked past her behind the front row seats until he was behind Renee. "What are you doing here?" The gruffness of his voice earned him a frown from Jack.

"We're here for moral support," she said, oblivious to or, more likely, ignoring his rudeness. She tilted her head toward Pastor Connor. "Although I see you've brought the big guns with you."

Cheerleader Renee in Oh-So-Professional Renee's clothes struck him speechless. Rhys looked from Jack to Suzi and then rested his gaze on Renee, drowning in the dark depths of her eyes. His voice caught. "Thank you. I can't tell you how much I appreciate it."

"I think your attorney needs to talk with you," Renee said, ending the moment.

"Right." He sidestepped to the aisle where Ms. Johnson sat.

"Let's go over to the side table," she said.

Rhys followed her. They sat and she pulled a sheet from his folder and pushed it toward him. "I know you received the conditions of the provisional custody Social Services recommended."

He had. He and the attorney had talked on the phone about them. Rhys ran his finger down the list: steady employment, safe living conditions, no association with former criminal contacts or with local known felons, no leaving the state with the boys without permission of Social Services and no relocating the boys outside of Essex County without review of the court...

Rhys pushed the paper back to her. He was an ex-convict, not an imbecile, although he'd certainly done some stupid things in the past. But that was the past. "I understand the conditions."

"Good. If the judge questions you, answer only what he asks. Don't add any other information."

"I understand," he repeated. Rhys could have

laughed. He was a man of few words to begin with, and one of the first things he'd learned as a delinquent teen was to never tell "the man" any information not specifically asked for.

"We're ready, then." She pushed from the table.

"It looks good?" he asked in an effort to calm the pod of dolphins doing backflips in his stomach.

"I can't give you any guarantees."

One of the dolphins did a triple spiral flip. She was supposed to be on his side. He studied her passive face. Maybe she was doing the best thing for him by not feeding his hopes. Rhys set his jaw and shook it off. He wasn't going to fail Owen and Dylan. Rhys glanced at Renee, Pastor Connor and the Hills. Nor his friends who had faith in him.

"All rise for Judge Richard Clark," the court clerk said as Rhys and his lawyer returned to their seats in the front row. The judge entered, took his place behind the bench. Rhys resisted wiping his hands on his pant legs.

After reciting the preliminary case information for the court record, Judge Clark called Rhys, his lawyer and the lawyer representing Owen and Dylan to the bench.

"Mr. Maddox," the judge said.

"Judge Clark," Rhys said with a respectful nod.

"Ms. Johnson, Mr. Richards," the judge greeted

the lawyers. "Is there anything not in the reports I received that you want to add now?"

"No, sir," they each said.

"Mr. Maddox, has your attorney explained the conditions of the provisional full custody the Department of Social Services has recommended, and do you fully understand them and the consequences of breaking any of the conditions?"

"Yes, sir." *Possibly losing Owen and Dylan for good.*

"I see no impediments to granting provisional custody of Owen and Dylan Maddox to their father, with a final custody hearing in three months. Social Services will transfer the children to you tomorrow. My clerk will give you the information."

The boulder that had been sitting on Rhys's chest rolled away as he watched the judge sign two copies of the custody decree. "Thank you, sir."

"You take good care of those boys. I don't want to hear otherwise."

"Yes, sir. You won't." Rhys's sight blurred. Owen and Dylan were his again.

"The court clerk has some forms for you to sign. Good luck."

Rhys nodded, not trusting his voice. He walked to the clerk and listened impatiently while he explained what Rhys was signing and where to sign.

He scribbled his name and the date and shook hands with Ms. Johnson and Mr. Richards. One more step completed.

Pastor Connor, the Hills and Renee met him in front of the courthouse.

"Congratulations!" Connor and Jack shook his hand as Suzi and Renee smiled on.

"Owen and Dylan will be thrilled," Suzi said.

Rhys could only pray that would be true. He and Dylan still had a long way to go.

Renee stepped up next to him and squeezed his hand. "I'm so happy for you. If you need anything, we're here for you."

He squeezed her hand back, and the cascade of emotions inside him collided and tumbled like the rapids of Niagara Falls. He appreciated the offer, but Owen and Dylan were his responsibility.

"Who wants to get some lunch to celebrate?" Suzi asked.

"Count me in," Connor said. "I'll treat."

Renee pulled her hand from Rhys's as if she'd just realized he was still holding it. "Sorry, I've got to go into the office for a new volunteer training session I'm giving this afternoon."

"I can't, either," Rhys said reluctantly. "Work." He'd told the supervisor on his scheduled job that he'd be there as soon as he could after the hearing ended. So there was no logical reason Renee's response should have stung, except that his nerves and emotions were totally haywire.

Rhys had thought he was as nervous as he could get yesterday. But yesterday didn't hold a candle to today. He wiped the sweat off his forehead with one of the work bandannas he'd pulled from the laundry basket in his bedroom. Maybe he should have unloaded the clothes. But there was no time now, as if Owen and Dylan would notice or care. He felt so much joy and excitement and, he'd admit to himself at least, fear at having Owen and Dylan here with him. They'd never even stayed overnight. He hadn't gotten beyond supervised visits with them. Now—bam!—they were his. Today. As soon as he got over to the Social Services' building.

Rhys gave the boys' room a final once-over. He'd gotten new racecar bedspreads for the nearly new twin beds he'd found at a garage sale soon after he'd rented the house—Owen had been so wild about his Pinewood derby car and all. He'd found and refinished a bookcase. Gwen had told Rhys about Dylan's appetite for reading. A duel-pronged pang of regret for what she would miss and remorse for what he'd done stabbed him. But it wasn't as intense as his previous bouts of regret and remorse. Would he have Gwen's forgiveness if she were still alive? *Definitely. And God's for-giveness, too*, his heart whispered.

Fifty minutes later Rhys raced up the walkway and into the Essex County building. He slowed his steps before he pulled open the door to the Social Services' office.

"Mr. Maddox," Ms. Bulmer said as he walked in. His gaze shot to the wall clock behind the sign-in desk. His stomach knotted. He wasn't late. No one had met him in the waiting room before. He'd always had to sit at least a few minutes before he saw her or Renee.

"Today's the big day." She smiled. "I have a few things to go over with you before Mrs. Hill and your sons arrive."

The knot loosened but the tangled strings remained. He followed her to a cubicle. The case-worker reiterated his custody conditions and set a date for a follow-up home visit in a week. He'd have to take more time off work. The ring of her phone filled the deafening silence that hung in the air after she'd finished talking, jarring his already jangled nerves.

"Yes, we're finished. Send her in." She hung up. "Mrs. Hill and your sons are in the family sitting area. Do you know your way?"

"Yes." It was the corner of the waiting room where he and Suzi and the boys had waited for

Renee the day Dylan had refused to go for ice cream with him. He swallowed. No, he wouldn't think about that.

"Good. My next appointment is here." Ms. Bulmer rose and offered her hand.

He shook it.

"Congratulations," she said, "and if you have questions, or any problem arises, don't hesitate to call on your support network. You've got a good one, better than many of the families I see."

"Thank you. I will." He left her, wondering if that had been some kind of warning.

"Dad!" Owen raced across the waiting room when his father hit the doorway.

Rhys glanced around the room to see if he should be reining in his son's exuberance, not that his wasn't at about the same level. But no one was frowning or even paying attention.

Owen pulled him by his hand across the room. "We've got all our stuff in Mr. Hill's truck. He's going to meet us at your house. It wouldn't fit in Mrs. Hill's car." Owen stopped. "If you don't have room for it all, there's some we could do without, like when we moved here with Mommy."

It pained Rhys that Owen and Dylan hadn't been to his house before and that they'd had to give up belongings when Gwen had moved them to Paradox Lake to be closer to him.

"We gave some, like baby stuff, to kids who don't have as much as us," Owen said.

That sounded like Gwen, making lemonade out of lemons. Except at the thought of lemonade, it wasn't Gwen's sweet face he saw in his mind but Renee's, apologizing for serving him canned rather than fresh lemonade.

"Don't worry," he said. "The house is bigger than our old one. You remember the house in Albany?"

From Owen's tentative nod, Rhys wasn't sure he did. "And our new house is just around the corner from your friend Alex's house."

"Get out." Owen stopped dead in front of Suzi and Dylan. "I could ride my bike there?"

Rhys bit the inside of his lower lip. When he'd gone away, Owen had just gotten his first two-wheeler with training wheels. Rhys glanced at Dylan, standing close to Suzi. Dylan could probably ride a bike now, too. He'd missed so much.

"We'll see." He'd have to talk with Anne and Neal about whether that was something they'd allow before he made a decision. "Hey, buddy," he said to his younger son, tipping his baseball cap back to see his full face.

"Hi, Daddy." Dylan gave him a shy smile.

"All ready?" he asked with some trepidation, hoping he had enough planned for the day to keep them busy, especially Dylan. He didn't want him missing Suzi.

"We're just waiting for Renee," Suzi said.

"Renee?" Had his voice actually squeaked?

"Didn't you get the email from the Building Bridges director?"

Not again. "In all honesty, I had so much on my mind yesterday that I never thought to check my email."

"The director feels having someone from the transitioning team—Renee—here could be helpful." Suzi looked down at Dylan. "Last time…"

He didn't want to think about the last time they were here. Didn't anyone but him see how far he and Dylan had come? Or was he kidding himself? In his entire life, he'd never questioned himself as much as he had the past few days.

"Miss Renee," Dylan called when Renee entered the waiting room. His face lit up when she walked over. "Mrs. Hill says you're going to come with us to Daddy's house. We can show you our new room, like when you were at the Hills and we showed Daddy our stuff."

"I am. Would you like that?"

"Yes," Rhys said in unison with his younger son, not realizing he'd spoken out loud until Renee chuckled.

"I'm a little nervous," he admitted.

"I caught that. We can do this. First up…"

Renee took over. "We need to head out to the parking lot and move Dylan's booster seat from Mrs. Hill's car to your truck. You have a bench seat, right?"

"Yep." That was one of his requirements when he'd bought the vehicle, a bench seat or an extended cab with a back seat like Jack Hill had.

Once they'd transferred Dylan's seat, Suzi said goodbye and left. Much to Rhys's relief, her leaving caused only a slight lip quiver from Dylan.

"We'll see Mrs. Hill Sunday at church," Rhys reassured him.

"And Grandma Hill will be at Kids Place when you start on Monday," Renee said.

Rhys smiled his thanks to Renee over Dylan's head. Monday, he and the boys would get a regular routine going. That would be good for all of them. He only needed to make it until then without any surprises.

From her parked car, Renee watched Owen and Dylan tumble out of Rhys's truck and scramble to Jack's pickup sitting in the driveway of Rhys's house. They pointed at their things in the truck bed and shouted to their dad. Rhys followed. She gave them a minute to blow off some steam. At the Social Services' office, all three of them had hummed with a combination of excitement and apprehension. Owen was more talkative than usual, while Dylan was quieter and more thoughtful. As for Rhys, if she had to guess, she'd say he was a man putting up a strong front. She pulled the car door handle. Time to bring in some reinforcements.

"The bike on top is mine," Dylan said as he climbed onto the bumper of Jack's truck.

A look of sadness seemed to pass over Rhys's face. Then it was gone.

"Hold on," Rhys said, lifting Dylan down onto the driveway. "Let Mr. Hill open the tailgate."

Jack pulled the tailgate down. "I know you've got two strong guys here to help you, but things are slow at the shop if you want me to stick around and help you after we unload."

Rhys's lips thinned.

Renee resisted stomping over to the truck. He wasn't going to refuse the help because he took care of his own, was he?

He broke into a smile. "We'd appreciate that. As Owen was telling me, they have a lot of stuff." Rhys reached for Dylan's bike.

"Miss Renee, are you going to help us?" Dylan asked when she joined them. "Mr. Hill is."

"I thought I would. I could use the exercise." She sensed Rhys's gaze on her and tugged the band holding her hair up in a ponytail tighter.

"Looks like you may be getting more exercise than you thought." Jack shoved his phone into his back pocket. "Dad just texted me that he got a tow call. I'm on duty until his shoulder heals. Mom won't let him drive the wrecker until she hears the okay from Dad's doctor. I'll help you unload." He and Rhys vaulted into the back of the truck.

"Owen and Dylan, Mr. Hill and I will hand the stuff to you and Miss Renee," Rhys said. "Put it on the grass out of the way so Mr. Hill can pull out when we're done."

"I'll take the heavy stuff for Miss Renee," Owen said.

Rhys cocked a grin. "Oh, I think Miss Renee can handle the heavy stuff."

Her pulse leaped. She focused on the truck tail-light. It was just an offhand compliment.

"And some of the heavier things will take two people," Rhys said.

"O-kay," Owen said.

Rhys handed Dylan's bike to her and Owen. Dylan took it from them and rolled it over to the grass. When she turned back to the truck, Jack was ready to pass off Owen's bike.

"See? Teamwork," Rhys said, his gaze lingering on her face.

Renee felt suddenly warm, beyond what she could attribute to her light exertion. But they were a team, part of the Bridges team. That's why she was here—as part of her job. Renee inched over to the side of the truck Jack was unloading, reasoning that the bikes looked like the only big, two-person items, and they could finish quicker if she worked with Jack and Owen worked with his dad.

A short time later Rhys jumped down from the truck and Jack handed him a large box labeled Books and Toys. Rhys heaved it onto his shoulder. "I'll take this right in, and then we can bring in the other stuff. Thanks for everything, Jack."

"No problem."

As Rhys headed to the side door of the garage, Jack approached Owen and Dylan. "Good work," Jack said, shaking each of their little hands. "Now you be good for your dad, and I'll see you at church."

Owen and Dylan nodded solemnly.

Rhys returned in time to wave Jack off. Had he purposely given his sons and Jack this time alone? A month ago, she wouldn't have thought it of him. Today she was pretty sure he had.

He eyed the random collection of things on the lawn. "Let's get this stuff inside. I'm getting hungry for lunch."

"Me, too," Dylan said.

"That's because he only ate half of the cereal Mrs. Hill made him for breakfast," Owen reported.

Rhys's eyes clouded.

She silently sympathized with him. He had to

have expected that both boys would have some apprehension about leaving the Hills', as she was sure Rhys did about having custody. "All the more reason to get this stuff inside so we can have lunch," she said.

"You guys take your bikes to the garage." Rhys had left the side door open. "Put them along the right side by the house."

"That's this side." Owen raised his right hand.

"I know that," Dylan said. "Can we ride them, Dad?"

"The lawn's kind of bumpy, but sure."

They hopped on their bikes and pedaled to the garage.

"I'll grab the backpacks," Renee said.

"Hmm?" Rhys turned from watching Owen and Dylan hop off their bikes at the garage door.

She lifted the backpacks.

"Yes, thanks." He heaved both of the boys' duffel bags over his shoulder. "It seems like I'm saying that a lot these days."

"It's okay to be thankful and to let others help." Renee wasn't sure if the crooked smile he gave her was an agreement or not.

Owen and Dylan met them halfway to the house. "We'll get the other stuff."

"Don't go by the road," Rhys called after them.

"We know."

Rhys pushed open the door from the garage to

the kitchen. "The problem is that I don't know what they know."

"You will soon enough," Renee said.

"I'm sure I will." He dropped the duffels to the floor. "If you want to take the packs up, their room is the one on the right at the top of the stairs. Through the living room." He pointed to the living room. "I'm going to make sure we got everything."

Renee stopped at the doorway to the living room. The gleaming pine floor was gorgeous, far too beautiful for a summer rental place that the house had been in recent years. The wood looked so recently refinished that she wondered if Rhys had done it. As she passed through the sparsely furnished room, she took in the sturdy, functional couch and well-worn recliner tilted to face the small flat-screen TV sitting on a wooden file cabinet.

The room was devoid of decorations save a picture of a younger Rhys with a toddler-aged Owen on his lap and an attractive blonde woman beside him, holding an infant Dylan. A paperback legal thriller lay tossed on one of the wooden side tables.

Definitely a man's room. And the room at the top of the equally beautiful wooden staircase was a little boy's dream. She smiled at the care Rhys had taken with it. But she'd come to expect no less from him than putting his sons' comfort before his own. Renee dropped the backpacks on the plush area rug between the twin beds and turned to go back downstairs. A rush of boys blocked her way into the hall.

"I beat you." Owen barreled in ahead of Dylan and came to a dead stop. "The cars on the bed look just like your old Charger, Dad—like my Pinewood Derby car."

Dylan pushed by his older brother and headed straight to the dinosaur-decorated bookcase. "Tyrannosaurus Rex. Miss Renee, I have a book about dinosaurs. Tyrannosaurus Rex is my favorite. And all my books will fit. I won't have to keep some in a box like I did at Mrs. Hill's."

While the boys' excitement filled the room to overflowing, it was dwarfed by the look of love on Rhys's face. Renee melted. Who would have guessed Rhys Maddox had that depth of feelings inside him? He placed the duffel bags beside the backpacks. His soft expression smoothed the sharp planes of his face and made him look more like the younger family man from the picture in his living room.

Her heart constricted. The man he was before his life had fallen apart.

Renee caught herself. Rhys wasn't blameless in that downfall. But as if a weight was lifted from her shoulders, she could fully accept that he'd moved beyond that life.

Rhys cleared his throat. "You guys pick which side of the room you want and start putting your clothes away." He pointed at two matching dressers by each of the beds. "I'll go get the box of books and toys." He ducked out of the room.

As if by silent agreement, Owen and Dylan chose the beds closest to their duffel bags.

"Miss Renee, can you help me open this?" Dylan asked after struggling with the zipper on his duffel.

"Sure." She bent and pulled the bag open. Her phone barked.

"What's that?" Dylan asked.

"My sister calling me." Claire had become so obsessed with finding their perfect dog that Renee had changed her ringtone to a barking dog.

"Hi, what's up?" Renee answered.

"Are you still at Rhys's house?"

"Yes, why?"

"We need that dog house sooner rather than later," Claire said. "I have our dog. A beautiful year-old Australian shepherd. My coworker's sister is moving and can't take the dog with her. Ask Rhys if he's free tomorrow to come over and work on the doghouse. I'll text you a picture of Precious. That's the dog." Claire clicked off and Renee waited for the text.

Renee and the two boys were huddled around her phone when Rhys returned.

"Dad," Owen said. "Miss Renee and her sister are getting a dog and she needs us to come and build a doghouse for it tomorrow. Can we get a dog, too?"

Renee straightened, knowing it was no use to even try to cover the blush that colored her cheeks. "I was going to ask when you'd be free to build the doghouse."

Rhys glanced from Owen to Dylan with a look that almost seemed to be one of relief. "Tomorrow is fine. Have you and Claire chosen a design?"

"Yes." She grinned. She was as excited about getting the dog as Claire. Or was it partly something else? She pushed away the idea that some of her feelings might be about Rhys coming over to build the doghouse. "We checked the plans you recommended online and like the 'Standard.'"

"Good choice."

She wasn't even going to try to figure out why his nice words made her insides bubble.

"Dad," Owen asked again. "Can we get a dog?"

"Ycah, can wc?" Dylan echoed.

"We'll see. But first you have to get moved in." Rhys motioned to the boys' belongings and they went right to work.

"And I'd better get back to the office," Renee said.

"I'll walk you out," Rhys said.

By the time they reached the steps into the garage, the silence between her and Rhys had gotten to be too much. "I certainly can give today a good report," she said.

"We're a report?" Rhys asked, sounding less than pleased.

Renee stumbled on the bottom step and he grabbed her elbow to stop her from falling. She was simply making conversation. There was no report. Why had she said that? That was one of the things she liked about her work with Building Bridges—she didn't have to write reports that had the power to upend Rhys's or any of her other Bridges' families' lives.

"No." She forced a cheery lilt into her voice. "But if you were a report, it would be a good one." She cringed before she looked over her shoulder for Rhys's reaction and caught his intense gaze. And blushed again at the totally inappropriate thought that filled her mind.

What it would be like to have Rhys Maddox kiss her?

Chapter Ten

"Is that a new top?" Claire asked, pouring herself a cup of the coffee Renee had put on when she'd come downstairs for breakfast a few minutes ago.

Claire made a show of sniffing the air. "And perfume?"

"Yes, the top is new and no to perfume. I used a new hair conditioner." Renee eyed Claire's cutoff jeans and oversize T-shirt. "There's nothing wrong with looking nice on weekends."

"Especially when a hunky man is coming over for the day."

"Rhys will be outside building your doghouse. I have things to do inside."

"So you admit Rhys is attractive."

"I have eyes. Even Meme thinks Rhys is attractive." Renee poured some Grape Nuts into her bowl of yogurt and stirred it.

"Meme. That's your backup? She's French and

admires all things of beauty." Claire laughed and stuck her head in the refrigerator. "Apparently those things you have to do include serving someone a steak dinner—a sirloin steak dinner."

Renee crunched down a spoonful of her cereal. "He did say he'd take his payment in home-cooked meals."

"I hope you bought enough steak." Claire popped an English muffin into the toaster and sat at the table with Renee. "Paul's coming to help, too."

The morning sunshine seemed to leave the kitchen. "You asked Paul to come over?" Renee ground her back molars. "To protect me?"

Claire scrunched her face. "What do you mean?"

Protect little Renee from herself. "Nothing." She was being childish. With her twin, Paul, so busy with the farm, it had been too long since they'd gotten together, except for coffee hour after church. Renee washed her cereal bowl and spoon and put them in the dish drainer. "I'll run out and get another steak."

"I can do that," Claire said. "Rhys will be here any time."

As if that was a major concern for her. But, uncomfortably, it was. Despite what she'd said to Claire, why else would she have taken so much care with her clothes and appearance on a Saturday morning? "No, thanks. Since you and Paul will be doing the cooking, I figure getting the food is my responsibility. Can you think of anything else I should pick up?"

"Do you have something for dessert?"

"I thought Owen and Dylan would like to go to the soft-serve stand on Paradox Lake for ice cream cones."

"Good idea, like Mom and Dad used to take us as kids after we helped Dad finish evening chores."

"Yeah, we always liked it. I'll be back in a half hour or so."

Renee gave herself a pep talk on the way down the stairs. She should be thankful that her twin was coming to help Rhys. The doghouse would go up twice as fast, and she probably wouldn't have to help at all with the construction. She could take care of those inside chores she'd told Claire she needed to do, whatever they might be.

When she returned, Rhys's and Paul's trucks were parked in front of the triplex, and laughter and conversation drifted out from the backyard as she walked around the side of the house.

Her nephew Robbie ran over to open the gate for her. "Hi, Aunt Renee. Uncle Paul brought me so I can help build your doghouse."

She waited while his little fingers worked the

latch then made sure it clicked closed behind her. "So I see."

"Me and Dylan and Owen helped Uncle Paul and Mr. Maddox carry the lumber from his truck."

"With all you strong men, you must have made short work of that."

"You're silly, Aunt Renee. Only Uncle Paul and Mr. Maddox are men."

Her nephew's correction pulled her attention to Rhys in his sleeveless athletic shirt and cut-off jeans, with a red bandanna tied around his forehead as a sweatband. There was no denying he was all man.

"Hey, Renee," Paul called. "I saw there was work to do and wondered where you were hiding."

"At the grocery store, getting another steak for you. I can take it back." Renee made to turn around. "Better yet, I'm putting you in charge of grilling the steaks."

"Beats trusting you with that, baby sister," Paul shot back.

Renee caught Rhys frowning at Paul. Was he defending her? She shook off that thought. Rhys was a self-sufficient guy, and she knew from her work at Social Services that he didn't have any siblings. Good-natured family bickering might be foreign to him. Or maybe he was impatient to get the work done.

"Don't mind Paul," she said. "We sisters have done the best we could with him."

Rhys schooled his face into a blank slate. She'd expected a smile or something. Renee tightened her grip on the plastic grocery bags. Why would Rhys feel he had to defend her against Paul? She had to get her imagination under control.

But the unanswered question was why she craved Rhys's defense.

For the next couple of hours Renee kept herself busy inside, marinating the steaks, cleaning, doing laundry, anything to stay inside and avoid Rhys until she got over whatever her problem was with him today. She needed to get back into their Building Bridges' mentor/volunteer mode they'd been in yesterday at his house before…

A little after one o'clock, Owen charged up the back stairway while she was putting the finishing touches on a tossed salad to go with the steaks. She'd run out of anything else to do inside. The guys had worked through lunchtime, telling Claire they were close to being finished when she'd offered to make sandwiches to tide them over until the barbecue.

"Miss Renee," Owen said, "your brother says it's time to put the steaks on. The doghouse is almost done. Dad is putting the shingles on the roof. You've gotta come see it. Your dog is going to love it."

Renee pulled the baking dish with the marinated steaks out of the refrigerator and took two trays from on top of the refrigerator. "Help me carry some of the food out and I will. Grab the bag of corn on the counter."

"Corn on the cob?" he asked. "It's my favorite."

"Corn on the cob. We can roast it on the grill."

Renee followed Owen out to the backyard, where Paul had the gas grill on and ready. She and Owen placed the food on the side shelf. Dylan and Robbie raced over, followed by Claire.

"Come on, Miss Renee, and see the doghouse," Dylan said.

"As soon as I bring out the rest of the food and the cups and plates," she said.

"I'll do that," Claire offered.

Renee hesitated. She couldn't hide in the house all day.

Dylan and Robbie grabbed her hands and dragged her to the doghouse. "It's almost done, except for being painted."

"Mr. Delacroix says we'll have to do that another day because we're all so hungry," Dylan said.

It took Renee a moment to realize that Mr. Delacroix meant Paul.

"And more than that," Rhys said with a sheepish look on his face, "we don't have any paint. I could say I was going to ask you and Claire what colors you wanted first, but the truth is I just plain forgot."

"Don't worry about it. You've had a few other things on your mind the past couple of days. Claire and I can paint the doghouse."

"We'll help you," Owen said. "Maybe tomorrow after church."

"Next weekend would be better," Renee said before realizing she was inviting them over for another day. "Let me take a look at this house." She stepped back and made a show of examining their work. Rhys, standing beside the structure, occupied her field of vision as much as the doghouse did. "Nice. The doghouse is very nice."

Rhys moved over by the boys. "Those steaks are starting to smell really good. We'd better get cleaned up."

"Can we use the hose like Mr. Delacroix did?" Owen asked.

"No, we'd better go inside," Rhys said.

Renee nodded, remembering what usually happened with her and her siblings as kids when they got hold of the hose on a hot summer day. Besides, their going inside would give her distance from Rhys.

She helped Claire set the picnic table, and Rhys and the boys trooped back into the yard at the same time Paul pronounced the steaks done. Renee let the others go ahead of her, and when she and Paul walked to the table, the only two spaces were between Dylan and Rhys and across from him.

"I saved you a seat," Dylan said.

She had no choice. Renee placed the disposable plate with her steak on the picnic table and slid in between Rhys and Dylan.

"Paul, would you say the blessing?" Claire asked.

Renee took Dylan's hand and felt Rhys's close around her other one. She bowed her head and closed her eyes. Her brother's voice, so like their dad's, took her back to the family dinners when they all lived at home. A mantle of familiarity and security blanketed her.

She felt a small loss when Paul finished and Rhys released her hand. But the spirited conversation they kept going throughout the meal brought the warm feeling back—except when her and Rhys's fingers brushed while reaching for the steak sauce at the same time, and the several times his knee bumped hers. Then her nerves skittered her into a less serene, if not less warm, place. She wavered between thinking the meal couldn't be over soon enough and wishing it wouldn't end.

When they'd all finished, Renee stood and

stepped back over the bench, managing to avoid any contact with Rhys. "I'll take the leftovers in while you guys clean up out here," Renee said. "You can use the corn bag for trash."

Paul saluted her, a holdover from when they were kids, and she stuck out her tongue at him.

"That's not the way to treat your elders," Paul cautioned the three boys in mock seriousness.

Renee rolled her eyes. "Seven minutes older."

She took her time getting back outside, singing along with the country song streaming up from Paul's phone on the picnic table as she put the leftover food and condiments in the refrigerator. Before they were thrown together again at the soft-serve stand, she needed a timeout from Rhys and the roller-coaster emotions she'd felt sharing the meal with him and his sons.

Renee bellowed out the refrain. Good thing her neighbors weren't home to be bothered by her enthusiastic, slightly off-key rendition. She closed the refrigerator door.

"Claire sent me up to see if you're about ready to go for ice cream and to get the trash bag from the kitchen. The bag the corn came in wasn't big enough for everything."

Renee snapped her mouth shut and spun around. Rhys was there. Right there.

"It's here." Renee pointed to the container under the counter beside the stove. "I'll…"

They both stepped and bent toward the container, brushing shoulders.

Renee looked up.

Rhys looked down. "There are one hundred good reasons I shouldn't do this, but I've been wanting to since yesterday."

The back of her neck pricked. It looked like she was going to get the answer to the pressing question she'd had recently.

He touched his lips to hers.

Renee leaned into the kiss long enough for it to knock all rational sense from her. When she'd managed to regain it, she pulled back.

Rhys looked at her with a soft expression similar to the one she'd seen on his face when they were at his house yesterday watching Owen and Dylan's reactions to the way he'd set up their room. Similar but different. It rocked her as much as the kiss.

"I hope that was okay with you," Rhys said, adding a crooked grin to the soft look still in his eyes.

"Fine," she said, in direct opposition to what her brain was telling her to say. *Better than fine.* "Tell Claire and the others I'll be right down."

He grabbed the bag and, whistling the tune now playing on Paul's phone, exited the back door.

So that's how kissing Rhys Maddox felt.

* * *

Six days. Rhys put the sandwiches he'd made in the small cooler. Six days since he'd lost control of his better judgment and kissed Renee. He tossed in three apples. Six days since he'd seen or heard from her. Rhys couldn't count Sunday service at Hazardtown Community Church, since she'd ducked out as soon as the choir had started the recessional hymn. He knew because he'd been watching her.

She hadn't been at the Bridges meeting at Kids Place yesterday afternoon, either. But the Building Bridges' director who'd covered for Renee had said she was with a child in her Newcomb group who'd had a family emergency. Rhys threw a handful of Oreo cookies in a plastic sandwich bag and added it to the cooler.

"Dad-dy." Dylan's voice from upstairs interrupted another replay of his impulsive kiss.

It had definitely been a thoughtless action, and he was paying for it with Renee's reaction—avoidance. Still, he couldn't say he one hundred percent regretted the kiss, only that it put him in Renee's bad graces.

"Dad-dy!" The volume of Dylan's plaintive call increased as he clomped down the stairs and into the kitchen. "Owen is wearing his Teenage Ninja Mutant Turtles shirt."

That was a problem?

Dylan huffed. "It's breaking the rules. Grandma Hill said we're all supposed to wear blue shirts to match our Kids Place hats so we don't get lost at the Great Escape." Dylan checked out Rhys's gray T-shirt. "I think you're supposed to wear a blue shirt, too."

He didn't want to encourage his sons to break rules, but this was the first he'd heard about the blue shirts. He didn't have a clean blue T-shirt and didn't know if Owen did, either. It was only a fluke that Dylan had found one in his drawer.

Rhys had only gotten a rundown of the details of the child-care center's end-of-summer trip to the Great Escape when he'd picked up Owen and Dylan after work on Wednesday. The college student hired to supervise Owen's older kids' group for the summer had "reminded" Rhys that the parental consent forms had been due that day. He'd hastily filled out the forms on the spot, not knowing how he'd missed seeing them before. He always went through both boys' backpacks every evening after dinner. Then, later Wednesday night, he'd found the forms and the parent information sheet fused together in a hard rectangle in the pocket of Owen's jeans in the dryer.

Owen joined them in the kitchen. "My shirt *is* blue under the picture."

"Looks blue to me," Rhys agreed.

"Does that mean I can wear my other blue shirt with the Tyrannosaurus Rex on it?" Dylan asked.

"Sure," Rhys said, "if you're quick about changing."

"All right." Dylan raced off. Both Dylan and Owen seemed to have two speeds—fast and faster.

"It's okay if you don't have a blue shirt," Owen assured Rhys. "My group leader said everyone should try to wear a blue shirt. But we weren't supposed to tell our parents they had to go out and buy us one. Dylan gets so hooked on following all the rules exactly. It's like he's afraid something really bad will happen to him if he doesn't."

"Breaking rules does have consequences," Rhys said.

"I know. But wearing a blue shirt isn't really a rule, like not running in the halls at school."

Rhys wondered if Owen had been called on that one. He closed the cooler. He was a prime example of what breaking too many rules could do to a person. But it wasn't the time to go into that, or the nuances of recommended actions versus hard-and-fast rules. Rhys understood what Owen meant, along with Dylan's fears. While he thought he was settling in well here in Paradox Lake, he still had times when he felt he was walking on eggshells trying not to break rules he might not be aware of. The days since he'd gotten custody of his sons were good examples. It seemed the other parents knew things he didn't.

He checked out Owen's shirt again. "I think your shirt and Dylan's dinosaur shirt are good compromises. They're mostly blue."

"That's what I thought, too." Owen studied him. "You don't have a blue shirt, Dad?"

"Not one that's clean. I wore my blue one to work yesterday." He only had six T-shirts total.

"Gray is close," Owen allowed.

"All ready." Dylan scooted into the kitchen with his T-Rex shirt on. "We're going to get our hats when we get to school."

"Yeah," Owen said, "they didn't want the little kids losing or forgetting them, so we don't get ours until today, either."

"Out to the truck." Rhys threw the strap of the cooler over his shoulder and locked the door behind them. The Great Escape was definitely a place he wanted to take the boys. With thirty other kids wasn't exactly how he'd pictured it, though. He'd rather go as just the three of them on a Saturday afternoon. Guys' day out. A scene of the amusement park as it was in childhood popped into his mind—with one major difference. He, Owen and Renee were walking between the attractions with an animated Dylan pointing out things to Renee, just like he'd showed her the completed doghouse last weekend.

Rhys brought his thoughts forward to the present and climbed into the truck. As usual, he double-checked to make sure the passenger-side airbag was turned off for the boys' safety and tried to get comfortable on the bench seat made more cramped by Dylan's booster seat. He turned the key. His vision of a day at Great Escape with Renee was pure fantasy, a longing for something he'd had and lost. The reality was that there was no room in the truck for the four of them to go anywhere together, and no room in his life right now for her or any other distractions from his parenting. And the more time he spent with Renee, the more of a distraction she became.

On the forty-five-minute drive to Lake George, Rhys told Owen and Dylan about the two times he'd been to the Great Escape and what he'd liked best. Despite the delay in getting out the door while Dylan changed his shirt, they arrived at the amusement park ten minutes before the nine o'clock meeting time. Rhys didn't see any of the others waiting at the designated spot by the entrance gate.

He exited the truck, and Owen and Dylan slid across the seat and got out the driver's side with him. It was easier than climbing over Dylan's booster seat, and Rhys always kept the child lock activated on the passenger-side door. He walked them to the meeting spot.

"Daddy, are you sure this is the right place?" Dylan looked at the people lined up at the gate. "I don't see anyone I know."

"I'm sure it's the right place," Rhys said. "We're just the first ones from The Kids Place to get here."

"Hey." Owen pointed at a car parking in a spot near Rhys's truck. "That looks like Miss Renee."

What would Renee be doing here? This was a Kids Place, not Bridges, field trip. "It's the same color and model as her car, but I don't think it's her," Rhys said.

"Yes, it is," Owen said.

Rhys's heart thumped. It was Renee. He watched her open the passenger-side door and let little Melody out.

"Hey, Miss Renee! Over here!" Owen and Dylan jumped up and down and waved their arms to get her attention, as if the shouting hadn't been enough.

"Hi," she said. "You guys the only ones here?"

Her greeting was friendly, not standoffish. Had he imagined she'd been avoiding him since he'd kissed her?

"Yep," Owen answered for him.

"We didn't know you were coming," Rhys blurted. *Swift.* Not "Hi, how are you?" or something else pleasant and conversational.

"Neither did I, until last night." Renee smiled at Melody, and Rhys wanted that smile for himself.

"Melody's grandmother unexpectedly got called into the hospital, mandatory overtime. They're short-staffed on nurses, and someone called in sick. Melody didn't want to come without her, and her grandmother didn't want her to miss the trip. She called me early this morning to see if I could come as Melody's special friend."

So he wasn't the only one from the Bridges group who called on Renee. Nor was he the only one she helped as part of her job. But, as much as he fought it, he was beginning to think he might want to be more than part of her job.

"You didn't come with the rest of the group. Most of them were meeting at the church and driving down together." Obviously she hadn't come with the others. She was here. They weren't. Maybe Bridges had a learning module on making conversation for tongue-challenged parents.

"It was easier to pick up Melody and come here directly."

Rhys shifted his weight, and Dylan saved him this time.

"Look, Melody's grandmother let her wear her blue Frozen shirt, like you let me wear my dinosaur shirt," Dylan said with a note of relief in his voice.

"I told you it was okay to wear a shirt with a picture on it," Owen said.

The way Renee smiled at Owen and Dylan reawakened the longing he'd battled earlier. He could deal with the frequent contact he had to have with Renee if he could limit it to contact as a family unit with others around, rather than one-on-one adult contact.

"Miss Renee," Owen asked, "did you get your doghouse painted?"

"No." She bit her lip. "We're not getting the dog."

Dylan rocked forward on the balls of his feet. "Then what are you going to do with the doghouse we built? Can we have it in case we get a dog?"

Renee laughed before he could reprimand Dylan. "We're not going to get Precious. Her owner is going to be able to keep her, after all. My sister and I are going to go to the shelter and pick out a different dog."

"Can we come with you?" Dylan asked.

"And paint the doghouse?" Owen asked.

"Guys," Rhys warned. "You're not supposed to invite yourself places." Spending another afternoon at her place wouldn't further his idea of keeping their contact to group things.

"It's okay," she said.

He held his breath for her to continue, but

Owen jumped in. "We can't paint tomorrow because Dad has to work, 'cause he took today off. But we can next Saturday."

"Maybe we should check that with your dad."

He released the breath. She was passing the ball to him. He searched her eyes for an indication of her leanings and came back clueless. "Yes, we can finish the doghouse next Saturday." He had agreed to do the whole job, after all.

"Can I paint, too?" Melody asked.

Yes. Melody and her grandmother. More people to distract Rhys from Renee.

"Sure, sweetie. I'll talk to your grandmother when I drop you off at home." Renee faced Rhys. "I have some things to do that morning, so why don't you all come over about one in the afternoon?"

"Sounds good."

"And then can we come with you to get your dog?" Dylan asked.

"That'll be another day," Renee said.

Rhys wet his lips. From Dylan's wide grin, his son had taken that as a yes. He should suggest they make the dog adoption a Bridges activity, during a regular Thursday meeting time. He could ask Pastor Connor if they could use the church van.

The entrance gate opened, interrupting the

conversation. The people around them began moving into the park.

"I wonder what's keeping the others," Renee said.

As if in answer, both of their cell phones pinged with a text from Karen.

Accident on the Northway. We're nearing the Great Escape exit.

A few minutes later, the rest of The Kids Place contingency arrived. Once everyone's admission fee had been paid, Karen Hill gathered the group and explained that the parents and special friends were free to take their kids off on their own or to stay with the teachers' groups. "We'll meet back here at two o'clock," she said.

"Hey, Dad, can I go with my friends and our teacher?" Owen asked.

Rhys bit back the no that sprang to his lips and stifled his disappointment. Owen was older and bigger enough that he'd want to go on rides Dylan couldn't go on. He'd have more fun with his friends, and that's what the trip was about— Owen and Dylan having fun, not him reliving one of the few good memories he had of his childhood and sharing them with his sons. "Sure. Mind your group leader and find us for lunch." He patted the cooler. "I have the food. Your leader can text me when you're ready to eat."

"Okay," Owen called over his shoulder.

"How about you, Dylan?" Rhys asked. "Do you have a friend you want to hang out with? We can hang out with him and his parent."

"No. I like being with Miss Renee and you. It's kind of like being with Mommy."

Rhys swallowed and stared at his athletic shoes. In some ways, it was how things might have been for him and Dylan as a family if he hadn't messed up. In other ways, it wasn't at all the same.

He'd loved Gwen. She'd been his wife. He and Renee...he didn't know what their relationship was beyond her being one of his "resources." But at least for him, he begrudgingly admitted, it was becoming something more. Who knew about how Renee felt? One thing he was sure of was that Renee would agree that they shouldn't let Dylan build up expectations about something that could wind up hurting him.

"Okay, buddy, then what do you and Melody want to do first?"

"Krazy Kups!" they both shouted.

"I've got it on the map," Renee said. "Let's go."

Five hours later, Rhys and Renee walked toward their vehicles in the parking lot with a wound-up Owen, a tired Dylan holding Renee's hand and an even more tired Melody drifting off in Rhys's arms. Renee opened the passenger-side door to her car and Rhys bent to fasten the now-asleep little girl into her seat.

He straightened to find himself gazing down at Renee, who was still holding the door handle, her upturned face taking him back to last Saturday afternoon in the kitchen of her apartment. Rhys quickly straightened to his full height. "See you at church tomorrow."

She cleared her throat. "Right, church."

"'Bye, Miss Renee," Owen and Dylan said, breaking the invisible tether between Rhys and Renee.

He and the boys approached his old beat-up pickup. Maybe it was time to look at a bigger vehicle. For Owen and Dylan's safety, of course.

Chapter Eleven

"Miss Renee, can I ask you a question?" Melody looked up at Renee as she opened the door of the post office, her last Saturday-morning errand done.

"Sure, sweetie."

"Is Mr. Rhys your boyfriend now?"

Renee choked down the water she'd sipped from her sports bottle. "Why do you ask?" She had no idea where Melody was going, but knew she should hear her out. This was the first time the little girl had started a conversation with her, rather than simply answering Renee's questions.

Melody pursed her lips, looking very serious. "Mr. Rhys built you a doghouse. And you went to the Great Escape with him."

"Mr. Rhys and I are friends, but not girlfriend and boyfriend."

Melody eyed her with skepticism. "Will, who

lived next to me and Mommy, was her friend and then her boyfriend. They went on dates. Do you and Mr. Rhys go on dates?"

Renee smiled at Melody's veiled way of asking whether she knew what a boyfriend was. Renee definitely did, and Rhys was definitely not.

"Then Will moved away and Mommy was sad like she was when Daddy went away. Would you be sad if Mr. Rhys went away?"

Renee's breath hitched. She sensed something more beneath the little girl's question, a sense that she couldn't trust in happy endings. "I'd be very sad if Mr. Rhys went away. But don't worry, as far as I know, the only place Mr. Rhys is going is to my house to paint the doghouse. And we'd better get a move on, or he and Owen and Dylan will be there before we are." She playfully swatted Melody with the mailing tube she'd picked up for Claire. The little girl giggled.

When Renee and Melody pulled into her driveway a few minutes later, Rhys's truck was already parked out front.

"They beat us here," Melody said. "Is Mr. Rhys going to be mad? Will used to get mad sometimes if Mommy wasn't ready to go when he came to get her."

Renee made a mental note to talk with Melody's grandmother about her opening up today and the little girl's concerns about people leaving.

"No, I'm sure Mr. Rhys won't be mad." The only times she'd seen him angry were when he'd thought his sons were threatened in some way. "I told him Thursday that if I wasn't back, the fence gate would be open and he could put the painting supplies by the doghouse."

When Renee opened the car door, Owen and Dylan were right there, ready and eager to get going. Rhys took his time ambling over.

"We've got everything set up to start painting," Owen said.

"That's great, but I need a little help first carrying in stuff."

She popped the trunk, walked to the back of the car and handed first Owen and then Dylan a bag of groceries.

"I can take two," Owen said.

"That's okay. I gave you the heavy one with the cans."

Melody walked around from the other side of the car, and Renee handed her a light bag with bread and potato chips in it.

"Wait for me at the top of the stairs," she said. "I'll need to unlock the door." Renee reached into the trunk and lifted out two more bags.

"I'll take those."

The rumble of Rhys's deep voice fueled her awareness that he was there. Right there beside her. She gulped a breath and relinquished the groceries with a smile she hoped didn't look as forced as it felt.

"You'll need your hands free to open the door," he said. "I'll get the others, too."

Of course, he was just being helpful. Not like he wanted to show her how big and strong he was, like his sons. She didn't need further evidence of that, anyway. His nearness made her acutely aware of his physical presence. And the loving care he took of his sons left no doubts in her mind about his strength as a man.

"Thanks." She scooted around him and strode toward the house. Within three steps, he'd grabbed the other three bags and caught up with her.

"Where's Melody's grandmother?" Rhys asked.

"Working. I offered to watch Melody for the day so she could help us. Why?"

He shrugged. "I thought she'd be here, too. And Claire?"

"She and Nick had plans. But I think the three kids will be enough of a chaperone."

Rhys made a strangled noise that could have been a laugh or a choke. Why had she said that? In the past couple of weeks he hadn't given her any sign he was personally interested in her, that the kiss was anything more than a reckless impulse. Her inner voice taunted her. *As if in-control Rhys Maddox ever does anything on impulse.*

"So we do need a chaperone?" he asked.

His words stopped her midstep.

Rhys had already taken the next step up, bringing him close enough that she could feel his heat and catch a spicy whiff of aftershave. For her benefit? She couldn't recall him wearing any before.

"It's a possibility," she said.

"I like possibilities."

"What's taking you guys so long?" Owen shouted.

"Yeah." Dylan peered around his brother on the platform at the top of the stairs, two steps away from her.

Nothing, except my legs seem to have turned to jelly and I need to get them working again to climb the rest of the stairs.

"Owen, we're right here," Rhys said.

Renee climbed the two stairs while Rhys told his sons, "You don't have to shout."

"They're just excited." She bit her lip. Her experience with Rhys was that unless he asked, he didn't like people managing him, especially when it concerned Owen and Dylan.

Renee unlocked the door and opened it for the children.

Rhys grabbed the edge of the door so Renee could go in ahead of him. "I know they're excited." He followed Renee into the kitchen and placed the grocery bags on the table with the bags the kids had carried in. "New things are exciting."

His blue eyes fixed on hers, causing a flutter of anticipation deep inside her.

"They've never painted a doghouse before." He grinned. "I've never painted a doghouse before."

And I've never felt quite this way about a man before. She pulled away and busied herself with the groceries. "I'll put these away. You guys go ahead and start the painting."

"Me, too?" Melody asked.

"If you want to, or you can help me."

Rhys held back for the little girl's answer while his boys barreled to the door.

"I want to paint," Melody said.

"All right. Go with Mr. Rhys, and I'll be down as soon as I'm done."

Rhys held out his hand and took Melody's tiny one in his, and Renee warmed at the sight. She knew the physical and emotional strength his grasp held.

A few minutes later, Renee stood on the platform at the top of the stairs, viewing what looked like three little acolytes painting the doghouse a bright blue. To protect their clothes, Rhys had cut head and arm holes in the white trash bags that they wore.

"Look, Miss Renee," Melody said when Renee

joined them. "I'm painting the whole back of the doghouse."

"And Dylan and I are painting the sides because we're bigger and there's more to paint," Owen said.

"I helped pick out the color," Dylan added, not to be left out. "Blue is my favorite."

"It's very bright and blue." She clomped down the wooden stairway.

Rhys shot her a lopsided grin that made her heart stutter. "A little more neon than the paint chip looked. I tried to steer them toward yellow to match the house, but I was outvoted."

"I see." Renee eyed Rhys. "Nice gear." Rhys, too, had on a white trash bag. It fit him like a second T-shirt.

"I have to protect my clothes while I'm painting."

"You need a smock, too, if you want to paint, Miss Renee," Melody said.

"I have one right here," Rhys added.

"All you have to do," Melody instructed her, "is lift up your arms and Mr. Rhys will drop it over you."

Renee did as told. The soft plastic slid over her. She poked her head through the opening and reached to tug down the bottom of the bag. Her fingers brushed Rhys's, who had reached toward her to do the same. He locked eyes with her and the air between them went thick and still. Rhys lowered his head instinctively, as if he might kiss her again.

But then he stepped back. "There you go. Ready to paint."

A cool breeze rustled her plastic smock and the leaves overhead. She needed to get her imagination under control. He hadn't been about to kiss her. He wouldn't kiss her here, not in front of the kids.

"Let's get to work," she said. "What do you want me to do?"

"You can paint the front and help me with the trim," Rhys said.

A couple of hours later, when Melody's grandmother arrived, they were admiring their work while enjoying the lemonade Popsicles Renee had made the night before.

"Grandma, look. It's all painted."

"So I see." The woman smiled a greeting to Renee and Rhys.

"I did the back, the whole back."

"Good job, everyone. We need to get going, Melody. We have a barbecue at my son's," her grandmother explained. "Say goodbye to your friends."

"'Bye, everyone. And, Mr. Rhys, I liked painting with you."

"I'll remember that next time I have painting to do."

A wide smile split her face. "Can I hug you goodbye?"

"You most certainly can."

"It's so good to see her smiling and talking," Melody's grandmother said in a quiet voice for Renee's ears only. "She's been especially reticent with men."

"You can thank Rhys's participation in the Bridges group for that. He's very good with the kids."

"I can see that. It's an important quality in a man. Come on, Melody. We need to go."

Renee waved goodbye. Was the older woman making a subtle comment about her and Rhys? Did she see them as a couple? Concern smothered the flutter that thought triggered. Thinking of Melody's questions earlier, she hoped the little girl hadn't said something like that to her grandmother. Rhys would not like his private life feeding the local grapevine—not that she was part of his private life.

"We'd better get going, too," Rhys said.

"If the boys want to help Claire and me pick out a dog, the North Country SPCA is having an adopt-a-pet event at the hardware store here a week from Wednesday. It's five to seven in the evening. If you give Kids Place your permission,

I could pick them up, and we could drop them off at your house afterward."

"No."

Her chest constricted with the fear that by extending her invitation in front of Owen and Dylan without clearing it with Rhys first, she'd overstepped.

"We'll all come. We can meet you there by six."

"Great." She watched the trio leave, smiling at the two boys mimicking Rhys's long-legged gait.

Renee couldn't remember the last day she'd had such fun, only that it was before her missionary work in Haiti. This afternoon, and the barbecue the other week, felt like coming home, and no matter how she tried to downplay it, Rhys was a big part of the reason. But was she ready to open her heart to the possibilities they'd both alluded to earlier?

All Owen and Dylan could talk about on the drive to Ticonderoga, all they'd talked about for the past week and a half, was dogs. Owen had found the SPCA website and the two of them had pored over the photos of the available dogs.

"Your destination is five hundred feet on the right," his phone GPS said.

"Now, remember, we can't get a dog tonight," Rhys reminded them as he made the turn.

"I know," Owen said.

"Maybe later," Dylan chimed in.

"Stay with me while we find Miss Renee," Rhys said when they got out of the truck.

"We don't have to find her. She's right there, walking toward us," Owen said.

Renee approached with a bounce in her step and a welcoming smile, seemingly as glad to see them as he was to see her. The waning sun behind her highlighted the arresting contrast between her creamy complexion and black hair.

"You look pretty, Miss Renee," Dylan said.

His son had stolen his unspoken words. "The man has good taste," Rhys said.

Renee's cheeks colored. "Thank you. The pets available for adoption are over there under the blue tents. Claire got delayed at work, so we're on our own."

That information didn't disappoint Rhys at all. The truth was that he hoped tonight would recapture the family feel of the Saturday they'd painted the doghouse, verify that it had been real, not just wishful on his part. He and Owen and Dylan were a package deal. Before he explored anything further between him and Renee, he had to be certain Renee was on board with that.

"Did you already pick out a dog?" Owen asked.

"No, I waited for you," Renee said.

"I checked the website and I think you might like Fancy or Colossus."

"Let's see if they're here."

When they reached the grass beside the parking lot where the tents were set up, Rhys let the boys go ahead, as much to have a minute with Renee as to take the edge off their excitement.

"Don't feel you have to choose one of the dogs Owen has picked out."

She grabbed his hand and squeezed it. "I know, and I appreciate your concern."

When Renee made no move to pull back her hand, he wrapped his around hers. The contentment that hummed through him blocked all of the noise and frenzy of the pets and the people checking them out. All he saw and felt was her beside him.

"I found them." Owen motioned them over. "This is Colossus."

The large, black Lab mix tugged at his leash and wagged his tail energetically at the sound of his name.

"May I?" She stepped closer to the dog.

"Yes, he's very friendly," the man holding his leash said.

Renee knelt and patted his head. "You are a handsome boy."

"He's great with kids, too," the man said.

Renee stood. "He may be a little large for

my apartment. I'm going to check out some of the others."

"Fancy's down here." Owen pointed to the far end of the tent.

Owen and Dylan led the way, while Rhys placed his hand on the small of Renee's back and guided her through the people milling around the pets. "He's a good-looking dog."

"A very large, good-looking dog, who'd be happier out in the country, like at your place."

"Whoa! As I told Owen and Dylan, we are not getting a dog tonight."

She raised her head toward the two of them, who were stopping to pet each dog they passed. "Those may be famous last words."

They caught up with the boys in front of a dog that looked like a miniature chocolate Lab.

"This is Fancy," Owen said.

In contrast to Colossus, Fancy sat poised, studying them, her tail slowly swishing across the grass.

"May I pet her?" Renee asked.

"Certainly. As you can see, she's very well behaved," the woman holding Fancy's leash said.

Renee knelt and rubbed the dog's head. Fancy rewarded her with a wet dog kiss.

"And loving," the woman said.

"I can see that."

"Would you like to take her for a walk?" The woman pointed to the grassy area behind the tent.

Owen and Dylan nodded like little bobble-heads.

"Yes." Renee laughed.

The woman handed her the leash and a plastic bag and scoop.

With the boys dancing around her, Fancy became more animated on the walk.

"Do you like her, Miss Renee?" Owen asked.

"I do, and Claire will, too. You did good research for me."

Owen smiled big, evidently proud of himself, and Rhys couldn't help the fatherly pride that welled up in him.

"We want Fancy," Renee said when they returned to the adoption tent. "I already filled out an adoption application online."

"Great, I'll pull your application up." The adoption volunteer walked them a couple feet down the table to the laptop set up there.

"Dad, while you're doing that stuff, can Owen take me to look at the cats?" Dylan asked.

It seemed safe enough. He'd be able to see them from here. "Yes, just both stay where I can see you."

"Okay, come on, Owen."

"Your boys are adorable," the woman said, more to Renee than him.

"They are," Renee said. "But they're not my sons. Just special friends."

Rhys shifted his weight and stuffed his fingers in the front pockets of his jeans. He wouldn't mind being Renee's special friend, too. But he was working on that.

Renee finished the paperwork, assured the woman that she had a crate in the car for Fancy's ride home and they joined Owen and Dylan at the cat cage and display.

"Daddy, Miss Renee, this is Midnight." Dylan snuggled the black cat in his arms under the watchful eye of a volunteer. "You said no dog, but can we get a cat?" He rubbed his face in Midnight's fur.

Rhys looked to Renee and she lifted her hands up, palms out.

He was on his own on this one. The expectation on Dylan's upturned face melted any resistance he may have had. "Yes, we can get Midnight. But you'll be responsible for taking care of it."

"I can do that." Dylan nodded.

"And we can still get a dog later, right?" Owen asked.

"Yes, once I've fenced an area for one." And got a little further ahead on his finances. Dogs could be expensive. Rhys studied Dylan and Midnight. Cats had to be cheaper, right?

"I'm going to take Fancy home," Renee said. "Thanks for helping me pick her out, guys."

"You're welcome," Owen and Dylan said.

"See you tomorrow." Rhys watched her and Fancy walk to the parking lot.

"Sir?" The volunteer who'd been keeping an eye on Dylan and Midnight prodded him.

"Right." Rhys pulled his gaze away. "What do I need to do to get the cat?"

Rhys completed the adoption process, then the volunteer put Midnight in a cardboard cat carrier and gave Dylan a cat goody bag, and they drove home.

Once home, Owen and Dylan pulled a jingle ball from the goody bag and rolled it across the living room floor for Midnight to chase. While they were entertaining the cat and themselves, Rhys paced the kitchen, working out a reason to call Renee that didn't sound too lame after being with her less than an hour ago. He finally gave up on finding the right line and just punched in her phone number.

After seven rings, he poised his finger above the phone screen, ready to end the call before it went to voice mail. It was a bad idea anyway.

"Hi," Renee said.

"Hey, you thanked the boys for helping you, but I never thanked you for inviting us. Ah— thanks."

"You're welcome."

Silence hung between them.

"Was there something else?" she asked.

"Yes." He swallowed hard. He hadn't done this in more than eleven years. "I was wondering if you'd like to catch a movie Saturday night. Just us." It wasn't smooth, but he'd gotten it out.

"I would."

It took all of Rhys's strength not to let loose with an Owen-like *All right!* "Okay, I'll check the listings and let you know Thursday what time I'll pick you up."

"Sounds good to me."

"'Bye." He collapsed in a kitchen chair feeling as wrung out as if he'd worked a hard twelve-hour day.

Owen and Dylan's laughter drifted into the room, reminding him of his commitment to them. *Lord, I pray I'm not getting myself into something deeper than I can handle right now.*

Renee checked herself in the decorative mirror in the living room. "Are you sure I'm not too dressed up?" She didn't wait for Claire to answer. "Maybe I should change into jeans."

"You're not too dressed up," Claire said.

She smoothed the skirt of her sundress. "We're just driving to the Marquis in Middlebury."

"All the way to Middlebury? Isn't the Majestic in Schroon Lake playing the same movie?"

"I…we thought it better if we went someplace

where we wouldn't run into a lot of people we know. You know how people talk. They'd have us engaged by next week."

Claire's eyes narrowed at Renee's attempt at being casual.

"Rhys suggested it. He's a private person and I respect that." *And I've gotten past any doubts I may have had that he's anything different from how he portrays himself—a hardworking Christian man who would do anything for his sons.*

"You're not overdressed, but you might want to take a light sweater. The nights are getting cooler."

Renee spun around in front of the mirror, making the skirt of the dress flare out and relieving some of her nervous energy. "Which one? The blue or the lavender?"

"The lavender one."

Fancy, who was sitting on the floor near Claire, barked her approval.

Renee stopped to pat the dog on the head before she hurried to her room, remembering Melody's innocent words about her mother's boyfriend not liking it if her mother wasn't ready when he came to pick her up. But Rhys wasn't her boyfriend. They were simply friends going on a movie date. Melody's question *Do you go on dates?* echoed in her head.

She yanked open the dresser drawer and pulled

out the sweater. Now she was judging the status of her love life with the measures of a four-year-old? A glance at her alarm clock told her it was five minutes before the time Rhys said he'd pick her up. She caught her breath to calm her jitters.

"Come in." Claire's voice carried up the hall.

Renee's pulse ticked up. Rhys was here. Early.

"How's Fancy settling in?" he asked, leaning down to pet the animal as Renee looked around the corner.

"As if she's always lived here," Claire answered.

"Hey." Renee stepped into the living room.

Rhys straightened to his full height.

Her breath caught for reasons that did nothing for her jitters. If she was overdressed, so was he. His light blue Oxford dress shirt brought out the blue of his eyes—eyes she'd once seen as icy—and somehow made his shoulders appear even wider than his T-shirts did. The shirt was tucked into a pair of sharply creased khaki pants. Brown Doc Martens were on his feet. All she'd ever seen him wear were boots or athletic shoes, even for church. Had Rhys gone clothes shopping for their date?

"Are you ready?" he asked.

"All set." She tore her gaze from him to pick up her purse and loop the sweater over her arm.

Rhys held the door open for her.

"You two kids have fun," Claire said.

Rhys's laughter echoed down the stairs to the outside door.

"What's so funny?"

"Claire. 'You two kids.' I'm almost positive I'm older than her."

She knew he was right. Rhys was thirty-three to Claire's thirty-one, and to her twenty-six.

"Too true," she said in a bright voice to lift the pall that had fallen over the already dim stairway, and to deflect him from thinking about their age difference. Would he think he was too old for her?

She turned the knob to the outside door and Rhys reached over her to push it open, treating her to the spicy scent of the aftershave she'd admired the day they'd painted the doghouse. She searched the street for his truck.

"Where did you park?"

"Right out front." A grin split his face as he took her hand and pulled her to the sidewalk— reminding her so much of Owen and Dylan in action—and over to a sleek black-and-chrome supercab pickup.

"This is yours? When did you get it?"

"I went looking Monday and made the deal Tuesday. It had to be driven from the dealership's other location in Vermont. I picked it up after work last night." Rhys beamed like a boy with a new toy. He unlocked the passenger-side door for her and took her arm to help her in. When he released her to close the door, his fingers left a warm imprint on her arm.

Rhys climbed in the other side. "Listen to that," he said as the engine roared to life with his turn of the key. "And I got a really sweet deal. Three years old, low miles. I posted the old truck's sale notice at the Paradox Lake General Store on my way home Tuesday, and a guy came by Thursday and bought it. He picked it up last night."

She rubbed her hand across the soft seat cover. "Nice."

"And safe, with more room for Dylan's booster seat. It bothered me having him and Owen in the front seat, even with the passenger airbag turned off. Now they can even have a friend ride along with us."

"You, too," Renee said.

He wrinkled his brow and she had to bite her lip not to laugh.

"Oh." Understanding spread across his face. "Say, a friend like you?" He smiled. "Sorry, I told myself this was going to be an adult night. I wasn't going to talk about Owen and Dylan. My new truck isn't a much better topic. I'm out of practice. I haven't been on a date in twelve years."

"I don't mind talking about the boys." She didn't. But their relationship, if there was going to be one, had to be based on more. She took a breath. "Change of topic. When we moved the boys in, I saw a legal thriller paperback on your living room table…"

During the rest of the drive to the theater, they talked about books and movies, their favorite scriptures, Rhys's job and his career aspirations, and their childhoods—mostly hers. The bits he shared gave her further insight into him, beyond being a father.

After they left the theater a couple of hours later, Rhys checked his cell phone and frowned. "I hope you don't mind getting something quick to eat." He kicked a stone on the sidewalk. "I told Kaitlyn, the college kid who's staying with Owen and Dylan, that I'd be home by ten. She works at a convenience store and has to open tomorrow morning at five." He laughed. "I can't remember the last time I had a curfew. Maybe never. Except…"

In prison. She silently finished his incomplete sentence. Her heart filled with compassion. That was far behind him. But a question she'd been carrying in the back of her mind slipped out. "How did you feel serving time for something you didn't do?"

He released a rough laugh. "Everyone at Dannemora maintains he's innocent. But how I felt was angry, stupid, ashamed, but most of all guilty for tearing my family apart. I did drive the getaway car for the one robbery, and I didn't serve much more time than I would have for that count alone. As awful as it was, it made me a better man. It brought me to Pastor Connor and God and to you."

Renee slipped her arm through his and squeezed it to her. "I'm sorry."

"No, you wanted to know, and it's part of who I am."

"Do you like Mexican food?" she asked.

"Yeah," he answered, accepting her abrupt change of subject.

"I know just the place."

Over fat burritos, they argued the pluses and minuses of the movie and its actors. For the drive home, they switched to football. She and her family were die-hard fans of Rhys's rival team. Before Renee knew it, he was pulling the truck up next to the curb in front of her house.

"Thanks. I had fun." She pulled at the door handle.

Rhys swung his door open. "You don't get away that easy. A gentleman always walks a lady to her door."

"I see." She looked up at the summer sky while she waited for him to come around. "Aren't the stars beautiful?"

"Hey, isn't that my line? The one before I ask you if you want to come up and see my etchings?"

Renee sputtered with laughter as he walked her the few steps to the porch.

"I had a good time, too," he said. "I can think of only one thing that would make it better."

"What might that be?" she asked, her lips parting.

"This." He slid his arms around her waist and lowered his head.

She lifted her arms to his shoulders and met his lips with hers, savoring the way they melded together.

Too soon, he broke the kiss. "So you wouldn't be against spending more time together?" His voice was a whisper in the night.

She reluctantly dropped her hands from his shoulders. "I can't think of any reason we shouldn't."

Chapter Twelve

"Ms. Renee, can you come and live at our house?" Dylan asked, making Renee almost drop the handful of glue sticks she was putting in the cabinet in her Sunday school room after class the next morning.

She placed the glue sticks in the plastic container in the cabinet, buying time to frame a response. "It's nice of you to ask. Any particular reason why?" Renee suspected Dylan was missing his mother or Suzi.

"To hug me when I'm scared."

"Doesn't Daddy hug you?" She couldn't imagine Rhys not soothing his son's fears.

"Sometimes, like last night, he can't." Dylan twisted the construction paper he'd carried from the table for her.

Ah. So this was about Rhys and her going out, his getting a babysitter for the boys. That was something they could work on in Bridges as a group. Most of the kids came from single-parent homes.

She took the paper from him and closed the cabinet door. "Let's sit and talk." They still had a few minutes before church service would start. Renee pulled out two chairs at the table, but when she sat, Dylan climbed onto her lap.

"Sometimes your daddy wants to go out with his friends, like when you go over to Robbie's to play."

Dylan nodded. "But I was scared later, after Daddy got home, when the scary man came."

Renee stiffened. "Tell me about the scary man." Then she relaxed. It was probably a dream.

"Hey." Owen appeared in the doorway. "Dad's waiting for you for service."

"Dylan's helping me clean up. Tell your dad we'll be there in a minute."

"Okay, we'll save you a seat."

"Did you dream about the bad man?"

"No, he was at our house. I woke up and went to Daddy's room. When he wasn't there, I went downstairs to make sure he was home."

Renee's heart squeezed at Dylan's insecurities. The little guy had been through so much.

"I saw Daddy and the bad man, so I stayed in the kitchen where they couldn't see me. The man was saying mean things to Daddy about money and a deal and that he was going to get him good, burn our house down with us in it."

By instinct, she tightened her arms around Dylan. Just before she had begun interning at CPS, there'd been an incident when CPS hadn't intervened fast enough with a similar threat, and a woman's ex-boyfriend had burned her apartment with her and her three children inside. The youngest child had been horribly injured.

"Then the man tried to punch Daddy, but Daddy stopped him and said he was going to call the police if the man didn't leave."

The weight pressing on her chest lessened. "Did Daddy call the police?"

"I don't know. I ran back to my room and hid under the covers."

"The police didn't come?" Rhys would have called them, wouldn't he? Or was he that wary of the law that he'd only threatened to call? The Rhys she thought she knew would protect his children at any cost to himself, even if he didn't fully trust the law.

"I didn't hear them come, and I was awake for a long time."

"Did Owen see the man, too?"

"No, he never wakes up like me."

She kissed the top of Dylan's head.

"Would you know the man if you saw him again?"

Dylan nodded. "He came to our house before and gave Daddy money."

Her stomach churned. What was going on? A picture of Rhys's new truck flashed in her mind, along with the new clothes. She swallowed the bile that rose in her throat. This was a child's version of what happened, and it contradicted what she and the Hazardtown Church community had come to know about Rhys. Or what they had come to believe about him.

Old doubts about him and the motives behind his faith pricked her. The last time she didn't believe and report something—the deathbed plea of the mother in Haiti… Renee's eyes teared up. That poor little girl.

"Miss Renee." Dylan tugged at her arm. "Can you take me to Daddy now?"

She would. Had to.

"Sure, let's go find your dad."

That was all she could do for now.

Dylan quickly spotted his family and pulled Renee along to join them. She was thankful the boy placed himself between Rhys and her. Her mind and emotions were too jumbled to risk an accidental touch of his hand or brush of his leg. She stood and sang the hymns by rote and sat and prayed for guidance. If anyone at coffee hour asked her about the sermon, she'd be hard-pressed to comment.

After the last hymn, she filed out into the aisle ahead of Rhys and his sons. But she couldn't rush ahead and ignore him, not after last night. Her instincts told her to talk with Rhys, let him explain away Dylan's story. Her professional side urged, *Wait, remember Haiti.* Could she trust Rhys to reach out to authorities for help? Her stomach twisted. Trust that he hadn't gotten himself involved in something he shouldn't be? They'd all trusted the father in Haiti. None of her praying during the service had told her which choice to make, only that she wasn't ready to talk with Rhys now.

He tapped her on the shoulder and stepped up beside her. "Good morning." Rhys's smile shot directly to her heart.

She forced a return smile. "Good morning,"

"Neal invited us to go fishing at the lake today. Want to come?"

Renee remembered the afternoon of her birthday when she and Claire had run into Rhys at the lake. His horseplay with Dylan and Robbie, watching the athletic beauty of him swimming out to the middle afterward. Yesterday she would have loved to join them.

"Sorry, I have other plans." *Right, like yard work.* "In fact, I need to skip coffee hour."

Rhys's smile dimmed in disappointment.

"See you Thursday."

"Right," he said.

No, nothing was right. Renee slowed her pace so he wouldn't think she was rushing away from him and so no one else would notice. But underneath her measured steps, she was running away again.

Once home, an hour-long walk, two hours spent working in the yard and an hour of housecleaning, interspersed with prayer, had brought her no closer to deciding what to do—talk with Rhys or make an anonymous call to Child Protection Services.

She dropped into the chair in the living room, tapped the Bible app on her phone and searched "protection," which took her to Psalms 12:7, among other verses. "Thou shalt keep them, O Lord. Thou shalt preserve them from this generation forever."

Rhys wasn't wicked. She knew that. The man who'd come to their house sounded as if he was. A photo from the *Times of Ti*, of the little girl hurt in the fire at her mother's apartment, imprinted itself in Renee's mind. Making the call could protect Rhys from danger, as well as the boys. She could see Rhys being wary of calling the police and believing he could handle whatever was going on himself. And she doubted she could convince him to report the incident, if he hadn't already.

Hand shaking, she went to the Essex County website on her phone and touched the report number. Her heart pounded with each ring. The automated voice mail picked up, and she swallowed hard. She was doing the right thing. All that would happen was that CPS would contact Rhys, investigate the incident and, hopefully, his caseworker could convince him to file a police report for all of their safety.

"Hurry up. I'm going to be late for work!" Rhys yelled upstairs, louder than he needed to.

He repositioned his ball cap. It wasn't Owen and Dylan's fault he hadn't slept well last night. He couldn't shake the feeling that something was off with him and Renee. Then Dylan had had a meltdown when they got to "God bless Mommy in Heaven" during their nighttime prayers. It was part of their nightly routine they'd brought from their time with the Hills. It had never bothered Dylan before, but last night he'd clung to him and tore at his heart by asking him repeatedly not to go away.

Even after he'd gotten Dylan calmed down and asleep, Dylan had woken up and come downstairs while he was watching the ten o'clock news. His son had said he couldn't find his stuffed T-Rex, but when Rhys had gone upstairs with him to look, it was right on Dylan's bed.

Rhys closed his eyes and released a pent-up breath. All he could think was that Dylan might have gotten up Saturday night and heard him arguing with Jay Clark, the guy who'd bought his old truck. But Dylan hadn't said anything.

Someone knocked at the front door. He'd been so lost in thought, he hadn't heard any car pull in. It had better not be Jay again. Rhys clenched his fists, thinking of Dylan's fears last night. As he crossed the living room, Rhys looked out the window. His Social Services' caseworker, Ms. Bulmer, and a man stood on the porch. This was a lousy time for a surprise home visit. Normally he would have already left to drop Owen and Dylan off at the before-school program at The Kids Place. He grimaced. He'd have to call into work and let the site supervisor know he'd be late. Neal had been understanding about the time he'd taken off so far, but Rhys knew the man had to have a limit.

"Good morning," he said, opening the door wide.

"Mr. Maddox," Ms. Bulmer said. "May we come in?"

"Of course, I was just getting ready to take the boys to the before-school program and go to work." Maybe that would help cut the visit short.

The caseworker stepped in, followed by the man. Another caseworker?

"Mr. Maddox. I have an order to remove Owen and Dylan from the house."

"What?" Rhys shouted.

The man moved between him and the caseworker. What was he? Her muscle? Rhys leaned into the doorknob he still grasped for support. No, the man was there to protect Ms. Bulmer from him.

"They're all ready for school. Couldn't I drop them off and then we could talk? You could follow me."

"I'm sorry. No. Suzi Hill will be here shortly to take the boys to school and pick them up afterward. We hope to have an emergency foster placement for them by then."

"Hey, Dad, we're ready." The boys rushed down the stairs and stopped short.

Rhys's whole being went numb.

The boys eyed Ms. Bulmer and the man.

"Daddy. You're not going away," Dylan accused. "You said last night you wouldn't."

Ms. Bulmer raised an eyebrow.

Dylan's words were killing him, but Owen's reaction was worse. He stared, expressionless. Owen was old enough to remember him going away before, to prison. Rhys shook it off. Whatever was going on, it wasn't as bad as that.

"I'm not going away." If they were placed back

in foster care, he'd still be there in Essex County and see them as often as he was allowed.

"Mrs. Hill is here," the caseworker said.

Rhys opened the door. Had Suzi knocked? He hadn't even heard. "Mrs. Hill is going to take you to school today and pick you up."

Relief flowed over Owen's face. "Do you have to work real late?"

A couple of times when he'd had to work past the closing time of the afterschool program, Suzi's mother-in-law, Karen, had taken the boys home and cared for them until he could pick them up.

"We have a big job to do today." That was true. He wasn't lying.

Dylan didn't ask why Suzi was taking them to school.

"Give your dad a hug goodbye," Suzi said.

So that he wouldn't frighten them, Rhys used all his strength to resist hugging them like he'd never let go. Over the boys' heads, Rhys caught a flash of pity in Suzi's eyes. He checked his anger. He didn't need pity. He hadn't done anything wrong.

"Come on." Suzi looped an arm over each boy's shoulders and whisked them out the still-open door.

Rhys closed it behind her. "What is this about?"

"May we sit down?" the caseworker asked.

"Be my guests." Rhys waited for them to sit on the couch before sitting in his recliner.

"We received an anonymous report that an incident of violence and threat of future violence took place here Saturday night."

The caseworker's words sucker punched him almost as much as her order to remove Owen and Dylan had. Who'd called? Jay? The man had been so drunk, Rhys didn't think he could have managed it, although he'd acted crazy enough to do it—for whatever reason.

"Is that true?"

Rhys breathed in and out. "You could construe it that way."

"Tell me what happened."

"The guy who bought my old truck last week showed up here about eleven Saturday night. I opened the door to him because I thought there might have been some problem with the truck. He'd said he worked nights. It was late, but he could have been on his way home from work."

Ms. Bulmer wrote on a yellow tablet. "Then what?"

"He was drunk or high. He started saying he was going to get me good if I didn't do some deal with him. He said I was part of some conspiracy to ruin his life, something about my boss, Neal Hazard."

"What did you do?"

"I tried to get him to sit and calm down, have some coffee, keep him off the road so he wouldn't hurt someone."

"You didn't think about him hurting Owen and Dylan?"

"I had things under control."

More writing. "The report said it was a physical altercation."

"Yeah, the guy took a swing at me. I blocked him, yanked his hand behind his back and got him out the door, which I locked behind him."

"Did you call the police?"

"I called 9-1-1. But all I did was give a tip about a drunk driver on Hazard Cove Road and a description of the truck. I thought I'd handled it."

"What's the man's name?"

"Jay Clark." Rhys pulled out his wallet and broke his long-standing rule of never telling anyone in authority more than they'd asked. "Here's the old registration for my truck if you want to run it through motor vehicles. Jay must have registered it Friday. He brought plates when he showed up that evening to pick up the truck."

"Can I take the registration?"

"I'd rather you didn't. The vehicle identification number is enough." He was probably being paranoid, but he didn't want to give away the only proof he had that he'd legally owned the vehicle.

She copied the number. "We'll look into the situation." Ms. Bulmer and her associate rose.

"Is there any possibility I'll have Owen and Dylan back today? This week?" He sounded desperate—because he was.

She shook her head. "These things take time."

"Can I call you and find out where they're being taken?"

"I'll be in my office until four. You can try to reach me and I'll tell you what I'm able to."

Rhys walked them to the door. After he'd shut it behind them, he put his head in his hands and cried for the second time in his adult life.

Dear Lord, what have I done? Renee stared at the phone on her desk in the Bridges' offices and went over the conversation she'd just had with her former boss at the Social Services' office. CPS had removed Owen and Dylan from Rhys's home. She'd expected CPS to do an internal investigation and advise more supervision for a time. Those poor little boys. Poor Rhys. He had to be devastated. She raised her gaze to the cross on the wall.

Please forgive me my selfishness in letting my need to assuage my guilt about not speaking up in Haiti to color my actions concerning Rhys, and give me the strength to face him as I should have in the first place.

Renee rose and gathered her things. She poked her head in the director's office on her way out. "I'm heading out. I need to pick up some paperwork at CPS for one of my Schroon Lake kids before the office closes."

"Sure. Have a good evening."

"Thanks." As if that was possible.

As difficult as it was, Renee ignored the text and call she received as she was driving to The Kids Place. She'd been waiting all day to hear from Rhys. When she checked her phone in the parking lot, both messages were from him. The text was terse—Call Me—and the voice mail almost as terse—CPS took Owen and Dylan. Call me. From the desperation in his voice, she knew "call me" really meant "help me."

Heart pounding, she called back and got a generic voice mail response to leave a message. "Rhys, it's Renee. I know. Meet me and Pastor Connor at his office when you get out of work." Her throat clogged. "I'm…we're here for you."

Owen and Dylan were ready and waiting when she walked into the church hall holding the CPS letter authorizing her to pick up the boys. They were the last kids left at the after-school program.

"Hi, Miss Renee."

"Hi, guys. Karen, I'm sorry I'm late."

"No problem. Suzi called me," the older woman

said. "Owen and Dylan helped me clean up and get ready for tomorrow."

"Is Daddy with you?" Dylan asked, looking behind her.

"No," Owen answered. "Don't you remember? He's working late." His eyes were wide with hope.

Hope that he'd given the right answer? That what he feared wasn't happening? Her chest burned with empathy and remorse.

"He's going to meet us and Pastor Connor here when he gets out of work. My sister Natalie, Pastor Connor's wife, is going to take you guys to the soft-serve stand to get a burger for supper and give us grown-ups time to talk."

"I know Miss Natalie," Dylan said. "She's our song lady."

"Yes." Renee remembered that last school year when the boys were with Suzi and Jack, they'd sung in the children's choir.

Pastor Connor stuck his head into the room. "Hi, we saw your car go by and walked over." He and Natalie joined them.

"Are you guys all ready?" Natalie asked.

Dylan edged closer to his older brother.

"Yes," Owen answered.

Natalie offered Dylan her hand and he took it.

Owen held back. "Miss Renee, you and Pastor Connor are going to fix this, right?"

"We're going to try as hard as we can."

He left with Natalie, and Renee and Connor went to his office to wait for Rhys. Renee filled him in on the details she hadn't given earlier when she'd called to set up the meeting.

A few minutes later Rhys thundered into the office. "What's going on? My caseworker told me to call before she left at four. I called three times, left three messages and got no call back."

"Hello to you, too," Pastor Connor said.

Rhys grimaced and shoved his hand through his hair. "Hello. Hi, Renee. Now, what's going on? You said on the phone that you knew."

"I do," she said.

"Why don't you go to the lounge and talk? I have work to do here," Pastor Connor said.

Renee's throat constricted. She'd thought the three of them were going to talk. "Sure," she choked out.

Rhys left the office first. She followed him across the hall to the lounge and took a seat by the low center table.

He closed the door. "What do you know?"

"Can you sit?"

"No." He started pacing between her chair and the windowed wall on the far side of the room.

"After Sunday school class, Dylan told me about the man who came to your house Saturday night."

Rhys stopped next to her. "Dylan saw us? I was afraid of that."

She nodded.

"That's why you torpedoed out of church." Rhys loomed over her. She understood he was upset, but she wouldn't let him intimidate her.

"Dylan was frightened. I was concerned for all of you. I prayed all day, and I did what I felt was right. I made an anonymous call to CPS's report line."

"Instead of talking with me." His voice reverberated off the windows.

"I truly thought all CPS would do was contact you, find out what happened, maybe schedule more home visits."

"Well, we both know that's not what happened." He dropped into the seat next to her. "You couldn't have asked me? It was the guy who bought my old truck. I didn't know he was drunk and crazy when I answered the door. I would never let anyone hurt my kids. He took a swing at me. I stopped him and threw him out. Then I called 9-1-1 and reported him as a drunk driver. My boys weren't in danger. End of story."

Renee tugged on a lock of her hair. "When I was in Haiti, I had a situation in which I made a wrong decision. A child was hurt. You have to understand. I decided to err on the side of caution this time."

He leaped from the chair. "I don't understand. Me, Owen, Dylan—all we are to you is a situation? I thought I knew you!"

"You do. I had to think of Dylan first. You would have."

"That's what I did. I threw the guy out. I took care of it."

"No, you didn't. You don't know what he's capable of doing in the future. Dylan heard him threaten to burn your house down. You should have called the sheriff's department."

A muscle bunched in his jaw. "So what now? Ms. Bulmer didn't call me back. I don't even know where Owen and Dylan are. This morning she said they'd be with Suzi, but only today, until CPS could find another foster family."

"They're with Natalie, having burgers at the soft-serve stand."

He sat back down in the chair, elbows on his knees, leaning toward her. "Explain."

"Your caseworker called me."

He interrupted. "She called you, not me."

"You violated one of the conditions of your provisional custody."

She could see his mind working.

"What did I do?" Confusion spread across his face.

"I don't know."

"Wait, how do you know the rest of it?"

"Because violating the condition means Owen and Dylan will be placed in temporary foster care until you have another hearing and..."

"Wait." The storm clouds that had filled his eyes since he'd entered Pastor Connor's office lifted. "Owen and Dylan are being placed with Natalie and Pastor Connor?"

"No, they're being placed with me."

The lounge door opened, saving Renee from facing Rhys's reaction alone.

"Daddy, you came back like you said you would." Dylan catapulted himself into his father's lap and hugged him tight.

"Of course I did."

Renee admired the way Rhys was automatically there for Dylan, to reassure the little boy. What would it be like to have him there for her, for comfort? She'd never find out now. Her decision based on fear and mistrust had cost her that.

Pastor Connor followed Owen in. "Sorry, they got ahead of us. Have you finished?"

"We're finished." Rhys's words were a double-edged sword.

"Then we'll give you a few minutes to talk with Owen and Dylan."

The bleakness returned to Rhys's eyes.

"Do you want me to stay?" Renee asked. She'd do anything to get herself, Rhys and the boys back to where they were before.

"No, I think you've done enough."

Renee blinked away the moisture in her eyes and stood to leave with Connor.

"When you're done, we can all say a prayer together," Pastor Connor said.

"That won't be necessary." Rhys pinned her gaze with his. "Prayer is what got me here."

The thought that she'd cost him his boys—and possibly his faith—shredded what part of her heart the sword had left untouched.

Chapter Thirteen

"I sold the man my old truck. How was I supposed to know he was a felon?" Rhys faced off with Ms. Bulmer at the lunchtime appointment he'd finagled the next day. Fortunately he was working at a site in Elizabethtown.

"You said you sold your truck to someone named Jay Clark."

"Right."

"Our investigation showed it was registered yesterday morning to a man with a different name, who is on parole for grand larceny. Until then, it was still registered to you."

Rhys pressed his palm to the table. "You think I lied?"

Her noncommittal expression shouted *yes*.

"Why would I have given you the VIN if I'd known it would cause me trouble? He paid for the truck. I signed the title and gave it to him. I didn't watch him fill it out."

"Was that your first contact with the man?"

Rhys held his temper. "No. I met with the guy three times—when he put a deposit on my truck, when he picked it up and when he came uninvited and I threw him out."

"You need to talk to your attorney about this. You met with the man several times in violation of your agreement. There's nothing I can do."

All traces of the encouragement the caseworker had given him at their last meeting were gone.

"Ms. Delacroix will contact you about visitation, and you'll be receiving a notice from Family Court."

Rhys took that as his dismissal. His pulse throbbed in his throat. He was back at square one with Ms. Delacroix and Social Services.

On his way out, his phone pinged with a text. It was from Renee.

Will you be home by five, five thirty? The boys need to get their things from your house. We could stop by the house after I pick them up from after-school.

He could be, although he'd said he'd work until dusk with a couple of the other guys. And lately he'd been taking advantage of Neal's generosity in taking so much time off for the boys. But more than that, he didn't know if he had the strength to be there for the opposite scenario of when he and Renee had moved the boys into his house.

His thumbs hovered above the phone's keyboard.

No. I have to work until seven in Elizabethtown.

Let her think what she might about him giving up an opportunity to see Owen and Dylan.

I'll call Ted and Mary Hazard and ask them to unlock for you.

Renee knew his landlords from church. It shouldn't be a problem. Rhys pressed Send before he changed his mind and said he'd be there.

The phone pinged again as Rhys drove to the job. Renee's answer? He'd check later.

Seven o'clock and the prospect of going home to an empty house came too soon. He could stop somewhere for food to kill the time, but despite the six straight hours of physical labor he'd put in, he had no appetite. The empty feeling in his stomach grew the closer he got to home. When the house came into view, an Essex County sheriff's car was sitting in his driveway.

His heart slammed against his breastbone. Something had happened to Owen or Dylan, or both of them. He took the turn into the driveway too fast, jammed on the brakes and jumped from the truck.

A deputy met him at the driver-side headlight. "Rhys Maddox?"

"Yes, my sons, what happened?"

The deputy's brow wrinkled as he flashed his badge. "We have a warrant to search these premises."

Every bit of oxygen left Rhys's lungs. "May I see it?" He forced the words out.

The deputy handed him the paper and a second sheriff's vehicle pulled in behind his truck. *Trapped.* Rhys shrugged off the old unwanted fear and read the warrant. Property had been stolen from his boss's worksites, places he'd worked at. Neal thought he was involved? First Renee. Now Neal. Where was their so-called Christian forgiveness for his past? Where was God? Why had he thought he could depend on Him, if no one else?

Rhys dropped his chin to his chest. Because God was all he had when he'd left Dannemora, and He was all he had now.

"Have at it," Rhys said. He had nothing to hide.

"We'll need a key to the back building." The deputy nodded at the large shed near the edge of the property along the tree-lined electric company right-of-way.

Rhys twisted the key off his keychain and handed it to the deputy. "It should be unlocked. My landlord said the lock is kind of wonky and I might want to replace it. Since I don't have anything in there, I didn't lock it."

The two pair of deputies split up, one heading out back and the other to the house with Rhys.

He unlocked the door and went in. "Okay if I get cleaned up? Upstairs?"

One of the deputies who was with him nodded, and they followed him to his bedroom. A deputy stood in the hall with Rhys while the other searched the room before allowing him to grab clean clothes. Then on to the bathroom, where the deputy checked the linen closet, the medicine cabinet and the cabinet beneath the sink and ascertained that Rhys would not be able to escape out the small octagon window and drop two stories for a getaway.

After his shower, Rhys stepped into the hall to face both deputies. One had his handcuffs out.

"Rhys Maddox, you're under arrest for grand larceny in the third degree."

The phone woke Renee from the doze she'd fallen into while watching the eleven o'clock news. Who would be calling this late?

"Renee. I'm glad you're up," Pastor Connor said.

"What's up? Natalie and the baby…"

"Are fine. But I thought you should know, for the boys, in case it somehow gets out. Rhys was arrested this evening."

She straightened in her chair. "For what?"

"Stealing construction materials from some of Neal Hazard's worksites. Rhys used his phone call to call me. I just got back from Elizabethtown."

"He wouldn't do that."

"I agree. But it looks bad. The sheriff's department received a tip on the thefts and searched the property Rhys rents." Connor lowered his voice, as if he didn't want anyone to hear. "The deputies found thousands of dollars' worth of stolen materials in the big shed in the back, and they have a security camera photo of his truck at the latest robbery last Friday night."

Hope fluttered inside her. "But he sold that truck Thursday. The guy picked it up Friday evening."

"It's his word against the evidence."

Renee gritted her teeth. Didn't Connor believe him? She did.

"DMV records show it wasn't registered to the new owner until Monday. Rhys's lawyer is going to try to get hold of the buyer tomorrow."

"Rhys has a lawyer? A public defender?"

"No, I called a friend from college. He's a criminal attorney in Glen Falls."

That information soothed her. A private attorney wouldn't let Rhys be falsely convicted, as the overworked public defender in Rhys's overturned bank robbery conviction had. Would he?

"Rhys is home?" she asked.

"No, they couldn't get a judge to convene Justice Court for an arraignment hearing until one tomorrow afternoon. He's in a holding cell at the Essex County Sheriff's Department until then."

A chill shot through her at the thought of Rhys in a cell, hearing the door clank shut behind him.

"Renee, are you still there?" Pastor Connor asked.

She cleared her throat. "Yes. You'll let me know what happens tomorrow afternoon?" The way they'd parted last night, she doubted she was on Rhys's list of people to confide in.

"Natalie and I are praying for Rhys and Owen and Dylan—and you."

"Thanks for letting me know. For everything." She didn't know why Pastor Connor was including her in his prayers, only that she needed them. Her conscience told her that she was partly responsible for getting Rhys into this mess. She had to find some way to fix it and—if it wasn't too late—to fix her and Rhys.

* * *

"Miss Renee, I forgot," Dylan said late the next morning as she turned into the school parking lot to drop him off after his dentist appointment.

"Forgot what?"

"It's my turn to bring the after-school snack today. I gave Daddy the paper before, before we had to come and stay with you. I don't want to get in trouble with Grandma Hill for not bringing it."

Renee turned the car around in the church parking lot. She was sure Karen would cover for Dylan if Renee explained, but Dylan was too upset. "We can run over to Tops before I drop you off and get cookies and juice. How does that sound?"

Dylan sniffled. "My favorite cookies and party punch juice?"

"Of course." Both Dylan and Owen were being stronger than two little boys should have to be. They got that from their dad. Rhys's inner strength was one of the many things she admired about him. But the boys and Rhys didn't have to go it alone. They had people who loved them. Renee gripped the steering wheel. People like her.

On the way out of the store, Dylan squeezed her hand and pulled her to a stop. "That's the man," he whispered, "the bad man who came to our house."

Renee followed Dylan's gaze to a man approaching the store. Jason Clemons. He'd worked for Neal, and rumor was that Neal had fired him for theft, although as far as she knew, Neal hadn't pressed charges. She moved to shield Dylan from the man's view, even though Dylan had told her he was out of sight when he'd seen Jason at the house, and scurried the boy to her car.

"You're sure that was the man you saw?" she asked Dylan as she checked his seat belt.

"Yes."

Rather than heading to the Northway after dropping Dylan off, Renee turned on Hazard Cove Road in the direction of Neal's house, praying he'd be there and not at a worksite or at the GreenSpaces office in Ticonderoga.

"Good." She breathed a sigh of relief when she saw his truck in the driveway. She hopped out of her car and went to his garage office.

"Hi," Neal said when she opened the door. "This is a surprise. Were you and Claire finally successful in talking your landlord into going solar to cut your electric bills?"

"No, only in letting us get a dog."

"Okay, then. What brings you here?"

"Rhys. Did you give the sheriff's department the tip that Rhys had stolen property—your property—in his storage shed?" She had to know where Neal stood.

"Absolutely not. Sit down."

Renee sat and told him about Rhys's arrest, what Dylan had seen Saturday night, Dylan identifying Jason Clemons as the man he saw at the house, Jason giving Rhys a false name when he bought his old truck and Social Services removing the boys to her house.

"That dirty scum." Neal slammed his palm to the desk. "Jason. He stole from me when he worked here, though nothing on the scale of the recent robberies. I caught him red-handed."

Renee's heart leaped. Would that information be enough to clear Rhys?

"I deducted the cost of the stolen materials from Jason's pay and fired him," Neal continued. "He was furious, thought I'd give him a second opportunity after taking the money back from his pay. I went out on a limb hiring him in the first place. He had prior robbery convictions. When Jason left, he threatened to make me hire him back, said I wouldn't find anyone in the area as qualified as him. And I couldn't—until I met Rhys."

"You'll help me clear him?"

"In a New York minute. Using the electric company right-of-way, Jason could have easily planted the stolen materials in the shed when Rhys wasn't home, without anyone seeing him from the road. We need to get to the sheriff's office." Neal stood and started for the door. He paused. "For another thing, at the time the sheriff estimates last Friday's theft took place, I was talking to Rhys on his landline about getting the boys together to go fishing on Sunday. I called him."

More hope blossomed inside Renee. "Did he say anything about selling his old truck?"

"Yes, that the guy who bought it had picked it up earlier, and Anne mentioned that she saw the truck at the general store during the time I was on the phone with Rhys. She got home just after I hung up and asked if I'd gotten hold of him, saying Rhys might be at the store. She didn't know he had a new truck."

"Rhys couldn't be in collusion with Jason," she said.

"No, he couldn't," Neal agreed.

Outside she said, "You go ahead. I'll take my car. I want to call Pastor Connor so he can get hold of Rhys's lawyer."

Neal roared off, and she called Connor.

"Renee, you just caught me. I'm on my way out for Cassie Reynolds's funeral. Is something wrong?"

"No, something may be right, very right." She explained and asked for Rhys's attorney's name and phone number.

Pastor Connor gave them to her. "I'll call him," he offered. "Are you and Neal on your way?"

"Neal left. I'm taking my car. I just need to

call my boss to let him know that I'll be late." Or not in at all, if things went well with Rhys. She closed the car door with a bang.

Regardless of how things went, she had a lot of things she needed to say to him, whether he wanted to hear them or not.

Rhys sat on a cot in the holding cell, waiting for his arraignment. Pastor Connor had a funeral this morning. His lawyer had court in Glen Falls, and then an hour's drive to Elizabethtown. So he sat waiting and praying—or, more accurately, thanking God over and over that Owen and Dylan and Renee hadn't been at the house getting the boys' things when he'd been arrested. As for his other attempts at prayers, the ones for guidance in doing what would be best for Owen and Dylan, he kept going in circles, uncertain if his thoughts were his despondency or the Lord answering him.

His insides felt scraped raw at the idea, but if he couldn't escape his past and make a good, stable home for his sons, maybe they'd be better off without him. If only he could be sure someone like the Hills would adopt them, he might be able to let go. His chest ached. If he faced prison again, he'd have to ask them—or Renee. He wouldn't allow Owen and Dylan to be bounced around the foster care system as he had been.

Now that he'd had time to think, he saw that

Renee had only done what she thought was best for Owen and Dylan, what he'd been trying to do since Owen was born and had failed at miserably without a partner to help him.

Rhys closed his eyes and tried to picture Gwen, him and the boys when they'd all been together and happy. Instead he saw him and Owen and Dylan—with Renee, moving the boys' things into the house on Paradox Lake.

"Okay, Maddox." Two county sheriff's deputies stopped beside the cell. "Time to go."

One of them slid open the cell door with a loud clang that shot through Rhys.

"Hands out in front," the officer said.

Rhys placed his hands in front. The deputy put handcuffs on him, and with the clink of them snapping shut, all feeling drained from his body, leaving him a hollow shell.

On the short drive in the sheriff's van to the county building, Rhys only felt numb. He was tired of fighting for a good life for Owen and Dylan, and now he had a backup plan to give them one if he couldn't.

"All right, out," one of the deputies said after opening the back door. The two deputies walked him into the building.

As they passed through the courtroom doorway, Rhys spotted Renee and Neal talking with his lawyer, Pastor Connor and the assistant district attorney. A rush of anger and embarrassment flushed out the numbness, putting his every nerve on end. He dropped his head and walked to his seat without making eye contact with anyone.

"Rhys." Greg Conrad, the attorney Pastor Connor had contacted for him, sat next to Rhys.

"Go ahead. Give me your worst," Rhys said.

"It's good," he said. "It looks like the district attorney won't press charges." He explained the new information from Neal and Renee.

Rhys's heart swelled to bursting. Renee and Neal had come to help him. They believed in him. No one had ever believed in him before, except Gwen, and after he was convicted of the bank robbery, that belief had rightly waned. As time passed, he'd realized Gwen visited him only for Owen and Dylan's sake, Owen's mostly, since Dylan had hardly remembered him.

Rhys raised his head. Neal and Renee weren't in the front of the courtroom any longer. He looked around. Nor were they anywhere else in the room. What had he expected? They'd done what good Christians do. They'd helped prevent a wrong. While he wished Renee had stayed, and longed for the opportunity to pursue the closeness they'd shared Saturday night, he couldn't expect any more from her. He'd always have the cloud of his past hovering above him. Like his sons, Renee deserved better.

The judge entered and called the court into session. "Mr. Conrad and Mr. Blake, approach the bench."

Rhys's attorney and the assistant district attorney walked up front and talked with the judge, then returned to their seats. He couldn't read either of the men's expressions.

The judge spoke. "This is the matter of Rhys Maddox, who is here to be arraigned today on grand larceny charges. Do the People want to say anything at this time?"

"Yes, your honor," ADA Blake said. "Due to new information regarding this case, the People withdraw the charges at this time."

"Mr. Conrad, do you have any objections?" the judge asked.

"No, Your Honor."

"In the case of the People versus Rhys Maddox, the request to dismiss the charges is granted." The judge looked at Rhys. "Mr. Maddox, you are free to go."

Rhys nodded his thanks, taking his first real deep breath since the deputy had placed the cuffs on him.

The deputy removed the handcuffs and Pastor Connor slapped him on the back. "The power of prayer."

"On that note, I can't thank you and Natalie enough for your prayers."

"I have a confession to make," Pastor Connor said. "I asked a select group of the church prayer chain to join Natalie and me. I hope you don't mind."

"I wouldn't have minded if you'd told the whole congregation, even those few who think Paradox Lake would be a better place without the likes of me." And he wouldn't have. There would always be people who would find him lacking because of his past. But through Christ, he felt secure for the first time in his life.

His chest tightened. If only he had Renee. No, he wouldn't go where he had no place being.

"Too bad they removed the cuffs," Renee said as Rhys and Pastor cleared the front door of the county building several minutes later.

Rhys stiffened.

Why had she said the first thing that had popped into her head when she saw him exit the building without the cuffs? Impulse had never served her well before.

"It makes it easier for me to kidnap you." She tried to lighten the tension between them.

Rhys rubbed his forehead, his expression distant.

Lord, stop me now before I make it worse.

"I'll catch you two later," Pastor Connor said, making a fast getaway to his car.

"So you want to kidnap me?" The smile that

tugged at the corners of Rhys's mouth shot right through her.

"At least until Owen and Dylan get out of school. I know a park in Schroon Lake where we can sit by a waterfall and talk."

"I seem to recall that we did that before, and it worked out."

On the drive to the park, Renee directed the conversation to Owen and Dylan, and Rhys didn't voice any objections. He lapped up the details of their past two and a half days like a man hitting an oasis after hiking a desert without water.

Renee parked on the side street next to the park. They got out of the car and Rhys touched her arm. "I got so busy talking about Owen and Dylan that I never thanked you for what you and Neal did."

"We did what any good friend would do for someone they care about." Renee grabbed his hand and laced her fingers through his.

"You, Connor, Neal. I've never had so many people who cared," Rhys said.

Renee led him to the chain-link fence along the drop-off to the small waterfall. The light spray cooled her face that was quickly heating. *Might as well lay it all out.*

"I more than care. I think—no, I know. I love you."

Rhys grabbed the fence hard enough to make

it and Renee's nerves rattle. "You do?" he asked. "Even with my record and everything that's happened the past week?"

"I love you. I know actions help define a man. The things you've done in the past, good and bad, have made you the man you are today—a good, strong, caring person of faith. A man any woman would be proud to love."

"I never...I didn't...I..."

Rhys stumbled for words and Renee's heart plummeted faster than the water rushing over the rocks of the waterfall.

He put his hands on her shoulders and leaned his forehead against hers. "I love you, too. Although I don't deserve it, I'm going to accept your love as the most precious gift anyone could give me and my sons, and I'll do my best to return it double."

Her lips trembled. "Once over is enough. I can be the baby brat my brothers and sisters say I am."

Rhys's chuckle reverberated through her.

She turned her head and lifted her face, giving in to the impulse to seal their love and their future with a kiss.

Epilogue

He'd had a lot of bad ideas in his life, but this one might be the worst. Rhys paced the Sunday school room and glanced at the Bridges kids and smattering of parents gathered there for the group's Christmas party at their last meeting before the holiday break from school. He rubbed the back of his neck. His intention was good, but he'd woken up this morning with the dread that his timing was all off.

Unbeknownst to Renee, he and Karen Hill had contacted all of the parents last week to invite them to the party to thank Renee for her hard work. They'd asked them to try to arrive with the kids ten minutes early, so everything would be in place when Renee got there.

She'd been in Atlanta for training this week, which had given him and some of the kids and parents the opportunity to decorate the room last evening, including the "chair of honor" Emma had dubbed the "princess chair." Emma and her mother had decorated the chair with an overabundance of artificial flowers and holly that Karen had found in the church storage closet.

He surveyed the room and counted the people. There were so many. He wasn't a people person. What had gotten into him? Rhys paced to the windows overlooking the parking lot.

"If the church has to replace the tiles on this floor because you've worn them down to nothing, I might have to hit you up for a special donation."

Rhys spun around. "Pastor Connor." His friend was the only person in the room besides Owen and Dylan who knew the additional honor he planned to bestow on Renee, although the honor would be more his.

He'd talked with Pastor Connor before he'd set anything up or even talked with Owen and Dylan. Connor had prayed with him on it, and Rhys had left Connor's office full of hope and excitement, without any doubts or the slightest twinge that what he planned was insane. But while he had no doubts, he had a lot of reservations that the venue was wrong, too public.

Pastor Connor joined him at the windows. "A little nervous?"

"More than when I was waiting to be cleared

of the robberies. Even more than waiting to hear on final custody of Owen and Dylan. Weren't you nervous?"

"Scared witless," Connor answered. "But I knew where to draw strength from, and you do, too."

"But what if she…?"

"Then there's a reason for it."

Rhys's nerves stopped sparking. He'd have to have faith. Trust the Lord with his future.

"Isn't that Renee's car?" Pastor Connor pointed out the window.

He swallowed. "It is." Rhys faced the room. "Miss Renee's here. Everyone get ready."

Melody and her grandmother were downstairs, poised to appear to have just arrived and would walk Renee to the room.

The children and parents, except Rhys and Owen and Dylan, took seats at the two tables set up for the party.

A few moments later Melody, her grandmother and Renee appeared in the doorway.

"Surprise!" everyone said.

A smile lit Renee's face and Rhys's heart as she took in the decorations and refreshments.

Rhys and his boys took over from Melody and her grandmother and led her to her seat. "As thanks for everything you've done for all of us…"

Rhys motioned around the room. "We have a special seat of honor for you."

Emma jumped up from her seat. "Mommy and I decorated your chair for the party. Isn't it beautiful?"

"It's lovely. But doesn't Mr. Rhys have a chair of honor, too?" Renee asked.

It was one more thing he loved about Renee— the way she always thought about and tried to include others.

"I wanted to make him one," Emma said. "But we ran out of flowers. Mr. Rhys said that was okay because the party's for you. But we all get to eat the Christmas cookies and have punch."

Renee settled in the chair, brushing the point of one of the holly leaves off her neck and drawing his attention to her delicate features. She was as beautiful outside as she was inside.

He cleared his throat. "Owen, Dylan and I have the honor of presenting you with this custom-made thank-you card."

Owen drew the oversize card from behind his back and handed it to Renee.

"As you can see, it's signed by all of us."

"Even me, Miss Renee," Melody said, loud enough to carry across the room. "I can write my name now."

Renee's eyes went soft with unshed tears. "I don't know what to say. Thank you all so much.

It's beautiful. But enough about me. I thought we were having a party."

"Yes!" the kids shouted.

"Not yet," Dylan said. "Daddy has more. Don't you, Daddy?" Dylan hopped from foot to foot.

"I don't know if I can take more," Renee said with a laugh.

I hope so. There was no turning back now. All his earlier self-doubts returned. Rhys glanced from Owen to Dylan as he fumbled in his pocket. As they'd practiced, they all went down on one knee.

Heart banging against his rib cage, Rhys looked up into Renee's eyes. "I love you. Will you marry me?"

"Marry us?" Owen and Dylan echoed.

"Oh." Renee placed her hand over her heart.

His heart stopped beating, and he almost dropped the ring box he held open toward her. How did he ever think a public proposal was a good idea?

Renee stood and opened her arms wide. "Of course I'll marry you," she said loudly and clearly, for the whole room to hear.

Everyone cheered as she hugged Dylan and Owen and held out her left hand for Rhys to slip on the ring.

"It's perfect." Her voice caught. "I love you."

He brushed his lips to hers in the briefest of

kisses and whispered against them, "We'll finish this later."

"I'll hold you to that." Her eyes sparkled. "Now, who wants to party?"

* * * * *

*Don't miss these other books
from Jean C. Gordon
set in the town of Paradox Lake:*

*SMALL-TOWN SWEETHEARTS
SMALL-TOWN DAD
SMALL-TOWN MOM
SMALL-TOWN MIDWIFE
WINNING THE TEACHER'S HEART
HOLIDAY HOMECOMING
THE BACHELOR'S SWEETHEART*

All available now from Love Inspired!

*Find more great reads at
www.LoveInspired.com*

Dear Reader,

Thank you for choosing to read *Reuniting His Family.* I hope you enjoyed Rhys and Renee's story and, if you've read my other Love Inspired books, returning to Paradox Lake and catching up with other residents.

We're all shaped by our pasts. In Renee's case, it's having grown up the youngest in her large, loving, extended family, and her experience doing mission work in Haiti. For Rhys, it's having been shuffled from foster family to foster family and his brushes with the law. Too often, we let pre-conceived notions generated by our pasts hinder the happiness our Lord wants for us. But, as Renee and Rhys show, with His help we can move beyond those notions.

To keep in touch with me, please sign up for my author newsletter at JeanCGordon.com. And feel free to email me at JeanCGordon@gmail.com or snail mail me at PO Box 113, Selkirk, NY 12158. You can also visit me at Facebook.com/JeanCGordon.author or Tweet me @JeanCGordon.

Blessings,
Jean C. Gordon

Get 2 Free Books,

Plus 2 Free Gifts—

just for trying the _Reader Service!_

Get 2 Free Books,
Plus 2 Free Gifts—
just for trying the Reader Service!

Love Inspired® HISTORICAL

Get 2 Free Books,
Plus 2 Free Gifts—
just for trying the Reader Service!

HARLEQUIN

HEARTWARMING

READERSERVICE.COM

Manage your account online!
- Review your order history
- Manage your payments
- Update your address

> ### *We've designed the Reader Service website just for you.*

Enjoy all the features!
- Discover new series available to you, and read excerpts from any series.
- Respond to mailings and special monthly offers.
- Browse the Bonus Bucks catalog and online-only exculsives.
- Share your feedback.

Visit us at:

ReaderService.com